Club Wicked:
MY WICKED NANNY

Ann Mayburn

LooseId.

ISBN 13: 978-1-62300-636-5
Club Wicked 2: My Wicked Nanny
Copyright © January 2014 by Ann Mayburn
Originally released in e-book format in April 2013

Cover Art by Fiona Jayde
Cover Layout and Design by Fiona Jayde

Printed in the U.S.A. by
Lightning Source, Inc.
1246 Heil Quaker Blvd
La Vergne TN 37086
www.lightningsource.com

CHAPTER ONE

Anya Kozlov pulled up to the imposing black wrought-iron gates of her new job and put her decrepit car into park, hoping it didn't stall out. Having to call a tow truck and blocking the entrance to the club wouldn't be the best first impression. Especially since her new position was with Wicked, an exclusive BDSM club in the middle of nowhere outside Washington, DC. It had taken her three weeks to go through the hiring process, even with a personal recommendation from one of the members and a squeaky-clean background.

She couldn't screw this up just because she was nervous enough to give a chipmunk on meth a run for its money.

Taking a deep breath and releasing it slowly, she let out a sigh of relief when her window actually went down on the first attempt. She pressed the button on the small speaker situated next to the gate with a trembling finger. Dormant rose vines climbed the side of the stones flanking the entrance, and she absently wondered what color they would be in bloom.

Probably black and red to match the club's style.

A moment later a woman's sultry voice came from the box. "May I help you?"

"Hi, my name is Anya Kozlov. I'm here to start work as a hostess, I mean waitress, I mean..." She struggled to think of the word that had been used to describe her job position.

"Server," the woman said in an amused tone. "Please follow the drive all the way down. The parking lot for the help is at the rear of the mansion. Mr. Florentine will be waiting for you inside."

"Thank you." She let out a relieved breath and shifted her car out of park, the engine whining as it chugged into a new gear. When the gates opened, she pulled through, following the long drive lit by beautifully sculpted brass lanterns on either side. The first hint of spring warmed the air, and little green buds graced the limbs of the mature trees as she passed. So far this didn't look like anything she'd seen online about what BDSM clubs were like. No cages swinging from the lanterns; no red-and-black flags lining the drive. She was actually rather disappointed by how normal it looked. Well, as normal as a mansion could be if you had a billion dollars in the bank.

She had to laugh at herself. Just because someone on a BDSM Web site said all BDSM clubs should be red and black, invoking a frightening feel, didn't mean it applied in real life.

Anya had been through the orientation course at the agency that handled the employment for Wicked, but that had been at an off-site location. No one was allowed to know where the club was or to visit it until all background checks and training were complete. This was the first time she would actually be allowed inside the club. The butterflies in her belly were going crazy.

During her orientation she'd received a crash course in some aspects of BDSM, but it was just a bare-bones understanding of the most basic aspects. Enough so that she could handle herself in one of the public bars at Wicked. If she decided later on that she wanted to be a server at a private bar deeper inside Wicked, where pretty much anything goes as far as BDSM was concerned, she'd have to go through an advanced training course. For example, if she wanted to serve in a high-protocol bar, she'd have to learn high protocol.

After all, they were hiring her as a server, not a club sex slave. If she wanted to indulge in the dark pleasures Wicked had to offer, any Master within these walls was more than qualified to train her to his taste. But in the meantime she'd better be the best damn server she could because she had a feeling Wicked wouldn't hesitate to fire her if she didn't live up to their high expectations.

For a girl from a small town in Indiana, learning a place like this existed had been a shock. Fortunately, Laurel, the woman Anya had interned with for the winter, was a member in good standing and was more than happy to fill Anya in on all the details. Laurel had told her that just like anything else in life, every Master and Mistress had different ideas on what made a perfect submissive, and most greatly enjoyed introducing an innocent young thing like Anya into the lifestyle personally. While Anya didn't know if she'd want to do anything with anyone, she had to admit the idea of some powerful Dom teaching her how to best serve him made her heart beat faster.

In the distance, through the trees, golden lights began to warm the night. As she took another curve, she caught a brief glimpse of the stone mansion; then the trees covered it again. When Laurel had first suggested the job, Anya had been sure it was for prostitution. Anything that paid three hundred to one thousand dollars a night for a server had to be prostitution.

Laurel had been appalled that Anya would think that; then she found it funny. After she referred to herself as a slave trader for three days, Anya had apologized and asked more about the club. The things Laurel told her... The decadence and the pure hedonism happening within those walls called to her. Some part of her soul, deeply hidden, stirred at the thought of being tied up, flogged, and made to orgasm over and over again. Of course Laurel also told her stories about relationships gone wrong and hilarious mistakes she'd seen newbie Doms make, but that didn't stop Anya from imagining all kinds of kinky things that might be happening inside the club, even if the thought of actually doing those things made her flush scarlet.

When Anya had left home to pursue her dreams, she'd promised herself that she'd never let fear stop her from experiencing everything life had to offer. It was that determination that had led to her scholarships, then interning with Laurel, and now on to a job at a fantastic sex club. If she could keep a grip on her anxiety, she could leave for her summer in Paris with money in her pocket and a much better understanding of both herself and her sexuality.

Slowing the car, she took a deep breath and tried to stop her hands from shaking. Really, she had nothing to be scared of. The security was insane, and her entire interview process had been extremely professional. She'd been told only 5 percent of the applicants were actually awarded a server position. The elegant woman in her late seventies who supervised Anya's hiring said she felt Anya had that certain spark that the members of Wicked would enjoy.

Whatever the heck that meant.

Anxiety spiked through her system as she made the final turn and let her foot off the gas, coasting toward the most amazing mansion she'd ever seen. The last remnants of twilight turned the sky a lovely purple-blue color, making a wonderful canvas for the stone building. Four stories high, clustered with terraces and elaborate stone carvings and well lit by artistically placed lights, the mansion could have graced the cover of a fairy-tale book.

As she drifted closer, a handsome valet looked up and tilted his head. Even though he probably couldn't see her, she still avoided looking at him as she drove around the side of the building. Here the illusion of a private estate was spoiled by the vast parking lot. It was still early in the evening, so it was only half-full, but the cars gleaming beneath the lot lights were amazing.

Lamborghinis, Ferraris, and Bentleys sat in neat rows, each car costing more than her mother had earned as a seamstress in her entire life before she'd passed away. The sheer wealth overwhelmed Anya, reminding her how much she didn't belong here. She was a nanny, a creative arts student, a girl from corn-country Indiana. They'd take one look at her chubby ass and send her home. She should turn around now and save herself the humiliation.

Still, she kept driving until she reached the employee lot. This parking area was almost full, and although most of the cars were new and shiny, she was glad to see they didn't cost more than the house she grew up in. Oh, there was a scattering of Mercedes-Benzes and high-end SUVs, but nothing like the Bentleys and Ferraris out front. Pulling in next to a minivan with a soccer-ball decal on the back, she couldn't help but giggle and wonder what kind of soccer mom worked at Wicked.

She'd just stepped out of the car when a sharply dressed older man strolled up. In an odd way, he reminded her of her Russian grandfather. The man approaching her had thick, neatly combed silver hair and warm brown eyes hidden beneath his heavy lids. His dark gray suit certainly hadn't come off any rack, and he even had a kerchief tucked into his breast pocket that matched his pale yellow tie. Confidence rolled off him in almost visible waves, but his smile was friendly.

"You must be Ms. Kozlov." His voice was cultured, elegant, and smooth, with a faint accent.

"Yes, that's me." Her voice cracked on the last word, and she swore he was laughing at her even though his face didn't move an inch.

"Welcome to Wicked. My name is Mr. Florentine. I'm good friends with Laurel, and she asked me to make sure you made it all right." He held out his hand, and she took a step away from her car to shake it. He had a nice, firm handshake. Strong, but not overpowering.

"Nice to meet you, Mr. Florentine. Any friend of Laurel's is a friend of mine." He gave her an odd look, and she decided to stick with being polite. Engaging in small talk was beyond her right now. She'd settle for not embarrassing herself any further.

She stepped back toward her car and reached into the passenger seat to grab her duffel bag with the scandalous excuse for a work outfit inside. It didn't surprise her Laurel had made sure a friend would take care of her. Though the other woman had no children of her own, she treated Anya like a member of her family, even if Anya was just a lowly intern. She swung her bag over her shoulder and shut her car door, hoping Mr. Florentine didn't notice the rust starting to creep around the bottom of the driver's side door.

Mr. Florentine took a step forward and held out his hand. "Here, let me."

She firmly placed her hand over her bag. "I've got it, sir. Please don't trouble yourself."

Now a small smile did turn the corners of his mouth. "Ms. Kozlov, I assure you it is not a problem. I'm an old-fashioned man, and I believe good manners dictate that a lovely young woman shouldn't have to carry her bag if there is an able-bodied gentleman nearby. I may be old, but I'm sure I can handle the weight of your bag."

Her cheeks heated, and she handed her bag to him. "Thank you, sir." There. She'd managed to remember one of the most important rules of decorum for working at Wicked: always address someone as Sir or Ma'am unless told differently.

"You are most welcome. Now if you'll follow me, I'll take you to Sunny, who will be the bartender that you'll be working with. She's a very sweet girl. I think you'll like her."

They walked through the lot, his presence making her feel safe even though he was a stranger. Something about the way he moved next to her was almost protective. Due to their height difference, she found herself taking two steps to his one. She cleared her throat and looked over at him.

"Have you worked here long, Mr. Florentine?"

He chuckled. "Yes, I've been with Wicked for a very long time."

When he didn't say anything more, she bit the inside of her cheek. What was she supposed to say now? She shoved her hands into her pockets, trying to keep from indulging in her nervous habit of twirling her hair. "It's a beautiful building."

He smiled. "What do you like the most about it?"

"Everything." He arched a brow, and she grinned up at him. The lights at the back of the building illuminated his creased face. "It reminds me of what I pictured Toad Hall looking like."

Mr. Florentine chuckled, a rich sound that echoed

through the rows of cars. "From *The Wind in the Willows?*"

Unsure if he was laughing at her, she nodded and looked away. "Yes, sir."

"I do hope I'm not Mr. Toad."

"Oh, oh no, sir, not at all."

"I was only teasing you, Ms. Kozlov. What is one of your favorite parts of the book?" He must have seen her confusion. "I read that story to my children around a thousand times while they were growing up, and my grandchildren ten thousand."

Hearing this sophisticated, urbane man talk about reading books to his children helped lessen her anxiety. "Hmm." She took a deep breath and tasted the promise of new growth and fertile earth in the air, a hint of the world waking from winter. "'Spring was moving in the air above and in the earth below and around him, penetrating even his dark and lowly little house with its spirit of divine discontent and longing.'"

"Lovely and very appropriate. I do believe there is more to you than what meets the eye, Ms. Kozlov."

"Oh no, I'm just a—"

"Brave young woman about to embark upon an adventure of her own."

"But—"

"Do not argue with me, girl." She jumped at the snap in his tone, the kindly old man gone and in his place a man who radiated control and power like a king.

"I'm sorry, sir." She ducked her head, cursing herself for arguing with not only an employee of Wicked but also a friend of Laurel's. Heck, he could even be some big-shot politician for all she knew. DC was rife with them. "I don't take compliments well. I... Well, my mother said vanity was one of the ultimate downfalls of women since Eve took a bite of an apple long ago."

He paused and turned to her, his profile half illuminated by the lights on the back of the building. "Ms. Kozlov, I suggest you find a polite way to respond to compliments rather soon. You, my dear, are going to catch quite a few eyes, and when a Master or Mistress compliments you, they are apt to take you over their knee for a spanking if you try to deny it."

"Seriously?" Her voice came out in an undignified squeak, real fear worming its way into her bones. "They can just grab me if they wish?"

"Of course not." He shifted her bag to his other arm. "Nothing and no one touches you without your permission. If they try, find someone with a pin like this in gold, or let one of the other servers know and they'll find a DM for you." He lifted his tie tack, and upon closer inspection, she saw it was a stylized *W* in the middle of a rather roman-looking sunburst.

"DM?" She remembered that phrase from her training and smiled. "Oh, you mean the dungeon monitors?"

"Correct. They are like the police of the club. They keep the submissives safe from the Doms and the Doms safe from the submissives." He winked, then began walking again. "Despite what you may think, I can assure you that submissives can indeed be just as dangerous as the Dominants but in a different way."

"Huh."

They reached the back of the building, and Mr. Florentine paused before reaching for the door. "Ms. Kozlov, this job is whatever you make of it. If you wish to simply work as a server, no one will think any less of you. However, if you wish to explore the delights Wicked has to offer... Well, let's say if I'd found a place like this when I was your age, I would have taken advantage of every opportunity offered to me. They would have had to drag me away from the club, unconscious, after a hell of a fight."

She giggled, taken in by his charm. "I'll keep that in mind, Mr. Florentine."

He smiled and knocked on the door. A moment later a huge man with flaming red hair and wearing a dark suit opened it, then bowed to Mr. Florentine. "Welcome back, Mr.

Florentine."

"Thank you, Barry. Ms. Kozlov is charming, and it was nice to stretch my legs."

The big man let out a sigh of relief and smiled at her. "Welcome, Ms. Kozlov. I'll take you to your trainer, Sunny."

Mr. Florentine handed her bag to her. "I do hope you enjoy your time at Wicked, Ms. Kozlov. Laurel highly recommended you, and I have to say that as always, she has the most excellent taste."

Looking down, she wished just once she wouldn't blush every time someone complimented her. "Thank you again, sir."

Barry chuckled. "Look at that blush. The Doms are going to love her."

Mr. Florentine laughed as well and headed down the hall to their left. Anya watched his retreating figure and wished he'd stayed with her a little bit longer. So far he was the only person she knew here.

"Ms. Kozlov, if you would please follow me."

Barry led her through a series of utilitarian hallways that clearly indicated this was the working area of the mansion. While still stylish, it certainly had none of the splendor the outside of the club suggested. Not that she'd been expecting crystal chandeliers hanging from the ceiling in the kitchen, but she was eager to see the grandeur Laurel had described.

Barry smiled down at her. "Nervous?"

"Yes, Sir." She took a deep breath and shifted her bag.

"I'll let you in on a secret. On my first day here I was so tense I hardly spoke two words to anyone. Some of the members thought I was mute and used sign language to try to talk with me."

That startled a laugh out of her, and the band of tension in her limbs eased slightly. "I'm afraid that will happen to me once I start work."

Barry stopped and knocked on a door with the word

Ladies Only above it. "You'll be fine. Sunny is a very sweet girl. Just listen to what she says and try to remember to speak."

A moment later the door opened, and a tall young woman with a dark pixie cut smiled at Anya with genuine warmth. Something about her cupid-bow lips and big brown eyes reminded Anya of silent movie stars from the 1920s. The girl on the other side of the door wore a pair of thigh-high red latex boots that complemented her long legs. Tiny shorts of the same material hugged her slim hips, and a matching red bra completed the outfit. While Anya had seen plenty of naked women when she worked sewing costumes at plays, she'd never seen a woman in such a provocative outfit.

"Hi! My name is Sunny, and I'm your trainer." She grabbed Anya in a quick hug and kissed both her cheeks before releasing her. "I'm so excited to see you."

Anya smiled back and tried to keep her gaze on Sunny's face. "Thank you. I'm very glad to be here."

Barry bowed to them both. "If you ladies will excuse me, I have a cranky chef I need to go deal with."

Sunny laughed. "Oh, dear. Did someone dare to suggest he make a cheeseburger for them?"

"Worse. They asked if we had any ketchup."

He waved, and Sunny took Anya's hand and tugged her through the doorway. "So, are you freaking out yet?"

Anya laughed and looked around a small lounge area with a cream sofa and chairs scattered around a glass table. Antique-looking brass lanterns gave the room a warm and comfortable feel with their dim lighting. "A little bit."

Sunny took a seat on one of the chairs, then crossed her long legs. "Sit down. I wanted to give you a chance to ask any questions before we enter the madness that is the women's locker room behind me. And don't worry about offending me or anything. It's better to ask a foolish question now than to do something stupid out of ignorance later. I'm sure they went over all of the server stuff during your training, but I bet you still have a lot of questions."

The other woman's energy was contagious, and Anya found some of her earlier excitement returning. "I guess my first question would be my costume. I brought something, but I'm not sure if it's the right thing to wear."

"You mean you aren't sure if you look slutty enough like *moi*?" Sunny giggled. "Don't worry. You can wear pretty much anything as long as it's flattering. We have one server who only wears evening gowns, another who favors skanky cheerleader outfits, and yet another who wears elaborate ball gowns. Then we have our Mistress bartenders and servers that always dress to the nines. And I can't forget Sister Immaculate, who usually wears some type of nun getup."

"A nun? For real?"

"Oh yeah. Lots of guys find it hot. You know, corrupting an innocent and all that." Sunny tapped her foot against the edge of the table. "Why don't you show me what you have and we'll go from there. If you need anything extra, there are some girls that are your height and size you can borrow from."

The word "size" made her all the more self-conscious about being a size 14 instead of what had to be a size 4 like Sunny. "Okay."

Anya picked her bag up off the floor and set it on the table. The first item she took out was a long, flowing robe of diaphanous gray material that had a pearl-like shimmer. She'd seen a similar one Laurel had made for a friend in gold, but the silver flattered her pale skin and hair better than the warm color.

"Ohhhh, pretty," Sunny said as she leaned forward and fingered the material. "Soft too. Kinda like silk."

Emboldened, Anya took out a baby-doll top made of the same material but with sparkly silver beading along the bodice to hide her nipples. The top was long enough to reach her upper thighs, so she hadn't brought an additional skirt. At the time she'd thought her outfit was extremely risqué, but now, looking at Sunny in her barely there clothes, she worried maybe she would be too covered.

"What do you think?"

"Honestly?"

"Yes, please."

"Just like any other place in the world, the more skin you show, the better the tips. I'd leave that lovely robe off and wear the negligee."

Discomfort twisted her stomach, mixing with her unease in a sour ball. "But they'll be able to see my underwear."

"Honey, that's nothing. Even though you'll be in the public portion of the bar tonight, there will be half-naked and sometimes fully naked people everywhere."

"Seriously?"

Sunny giggled. "Yes, seriously. You'll be helping me at the bar. Did you bring any shoes?"

Anya fished out a pair of high heels she'd only worn once. "I have these and a pair of ballet flats."

"Are you used to walking in heels? You're going to be on your feet for a good six hours tonight, taking drinks from the bar to the members in the lounge area. I don't want you to cripple yourself on your first night. I mean, if you have experience walking around in high heels for your day job, you might be okay. Otherwise I'd stick to the ballet flats."

She sighed. "No. My daytime job is as a nanny. High heels and spirited children don't mix."

"You know, I can totally picture it. You have this very calm, peaceful aura about you. Bet you're great with kids." Sunny pursed her lips. "The ballet flats will work, and I think Vivienne has some slave bells we can put around your ankles. Then we'll probably need a mask for you as well."

"Why?"

"Almost all of the servers and bartenders wear masks, as well as a bunch of the members. It helps protect our identity and gives the members a sense of privacy. If they saw you out and about in the real world, they would never know who you are, so there wouldn't be any weirdness. Not that it really matters anyways. Those privacy contracts we all have to sign pretty much ensure no one ever talks about Wicked."

"That makes sense. Should I pick a fake name as well? I mean, Anya isn't very common."

"Yes. Do you have anything in mind?"

"No, not really. I never thought about it until now."

Sunny leaned back and tilted her head, examining Anya with a shrewd eye. "How about Dove?"

"Dove?"

"Yeah. You're soft and sweet like a dove, and your eyes are a blue-gray. That pale blonde hair of yours adds to your innocent look. Plus, and most importantly, we don't have anyone who goes by that name yet."

"Dove. I like it."

"Excellent. Just remember to introduce yourself by that name. I'm assuming you're more submissive than Dominant?"

"Yeah. The idea of being in charge doesn't really do it for me. I have enough going on with my life without adding a needy man to the mix. Not that I'm looking or anything, but if someone asked me, I'd say submissive."

"Me too." Sunny grinned. "Besides, wait until you get an eyeful of some of the single Masters. They are so hot. I've seen Mistresses turn into slaves for the Doms of Wicked."

"Wow." She sighed and slowly folded up the robe. "You really think I'd look okay in only the dress? I'm not, you know, slender like you."

"Don't be silly. If there is one thing I've learned from working here, it is that men love women of all shapes and sizes. Excuse me for being frank, but with your big breasts and round ass, you'll have the single Doms sniffing after you."

The familiar flush warmed her from the neck up. "Thank you. Um, can I ask you a kinda uncomfortable question?"

"Sure."

"During my interviews I was told that after my shift was over I was free to use the club. I'm assuming that means I can, you know, do stuff with people." She darted a glance at Sunny, then back at her bag as she put the robe away. During orientation they'd told Anya having sex with the members was a personal choice, but now that she was here, she couldn't help worrying. "Are we...expected to...do stuff with members?"

"No. This isn't a brothel, and no one, ever, will make you do anything you don't want. If they did, Mr. Florentine would have their balls and their membership in a vise. And trust me when I say you don't want to fuck with Mr. Florentine, ever."

"I met Mr. Florentine earlier. He seems like a very nice man."

Sunny gave a startled laugh. "You met Mr. Florentine?"

"Well, yes. He walked me in from the parking lot."

"Dove, he's the co-owner and chairman of the board of Wicked. He's like the king around here."

"Oh. But he was so nice."

"Of course he's nice. Just because he's powerful and influential doesn't mean he has to act like an egomaniac. Most of the superpowerful guys here are also the nicest. It's usually the ones that are still clawing their way up the ladder who put on airs."

Anya thought about some of the actresses she knew and nodded in agreement. "I can see that. I'm going to school to be a costume designer, so I spend a lot of time with performers, some of them famous. I met a Russian prima ballerina who was one of the nicest people I've ever had the pleasure of being around, but her understudy was a real bitch."

Sunny looked over her shoulder at the closed door. "Speaking of bitches, be on your guard around some of the other servers. There are a few who can't stand any competition for money or interest from the club members. I'm not saying they'll try to beat you up in the parking lot, but they can be catty and immature. You know, like high school."

"Great. So I'll be dealing with queen BDSM bees?"

With a giggle, Sunny stood. "Don't worry. I've got your back. Remember you're here to make money and maybe have some fun on the side."

"Do you have any fun on the side?" Anya slung her bag over her shoulder.

Now it was Sunny's turn to blush. "Uh, no, I don't. At all. Like never."

"Never ever?" Anya looked down at Sunny's erotic costume and back up. "Ever?"

Sunny gave a dramatic sigh. "Yes, I'm a virgin."

"What?" Anya cleared her throat and tried to keep from hurting the other girl's feelings. "I mean, that's great."

"Don't give me that look." She grinned to soften the blow of her words. "I just want to wait until I meet the right guy. My mom, well, let's just say her own dating habits have soured me on casual sex."

Anya moved next to Sunny and gave her hand a squeeze. "I think that's lovely. And trust me when I say I so wished I had waited for the right guy. My after-prom sex for the first time was awkward at best. At least you know when it happens, it's going to be great."

"Thanks. Okay, let's go doll you up before we throw you to the lions."

CHAPTER TWO

Anya took a deep breath, forcing air into her oxygen-starved lungs. Dressed in her scandalous outfit, complete now with an ultrathin, beaded mask that obscured the upper portion of her face, she at least looked the part of a server. And hopefully the mask helped to obscure the no doubt stunned expression as the first glimpse of the interior of the public bar left her overwhelmed.

Anya bumped into Sunny's back, totally not paying attention to where she was going. The other woman turned around and caught her before she stumbled. "Oh, that's right. This is your first time seeing it."

Anya could only nod, speech beyond her. They were in a replica of the Hall of Mirrors in the Palace of Versailles. Arched ceilings painted with amazing frescos towered a story above them. The images were rather erotic. Rubenesque women cavorted in all manners of sexual play amid a beautiful sky. Anya took a step forward, and more of the room came into view. Immense windows looked out into an artfully lit garden, and enormous chandeliers dripped from overhead like frozen waterfalls of diamonds.

Sunny moved behind her and whispered into her ear, "Isn't it amazing? All this lush decadence, but you're missing the most marvelous thing of all. Look down and take a peek at how the top one percent likes to play."

Anya kept her gaze on the ceiling, tracing the contours of the arches, the perfection of the design. "You don't understand.

I want to go spend a summer in France more than anything in the world. My grandmother is from Paris, and I grew up with stories of all the wonderful things over there, including this room. I take some of the inspiration for my costumes from the architecture and—"

Sunny laughed, her warm breath blowing across Anya's ear. "Dove, look down."

She did, and when she got an eyeful of what was happening right in front of her, she gasped. While the upper half of Anya's face was covered by some amazing silver foam that conformed to her every expression like it was painted on, she was sure from the chest up her skin was a nice tomato red.

Sunny sauntered in front of her and leaned against the edge of the black marble bar top separating them from the crowd. She rested on her elbow, looking elegant and sophisticated. She wore a golden mask fashioned like the sun and set with thousands of tiny golden crystals covering the surface. "And this is the public bar. The bars further into the club are much worse...and much better."

Forcing a breath into her frozen lungs, Anya took a hesitant step forward, the silver bells around each of her ankles tinkling. Her gaze remained fastened on a totally nude man approaching them. "But he's naked."

She didn't like how her voice sounded breathless, but for the love of all things holy, a man with a very large erection was being led past them with a leash attached to a ring around his cock. Some pretty brunette was walking a man, like a dog, by his dick.

Anya couldn't believe she'd seen that, even as she followed his progress through the room. No one else seemed to be shocked, and when the woman stopped to talk to an older lady with her hair in a tight bun, the older woman fondled his butt like she had every right. Even more confusing, the man with a leash on his dick looked pleased.

"But...naked."

"Hmm? Oh yes. Earlier tonight the club Dommes had

their monthly meeting. We'll have a nice amount of male eye candy to drool over."

"But...*naked.*"

Anya didn't want to sound like a fool—well, any more than she already did—so she didn't tell Sunny she'd only had sex once with the lights on and even then hadn't really gotten a good look at her partner. Most of her sexual encounters had taken place in the shadows, where she didn't have to show her body. While in the dark, men seemed to prefer soft and squishy like herself, in the light they wanted the stick-thin supermodel. Now she could see all she'd felt, and it was mind-blowing. No pictures or Web sites could have prepared her for the overwhelming experience of being here.

Her brief training in BDSM provided by Wicked certainly hadn't.

Then again, how the heck could you prepare anyone for something like this?

The atmosphere was raw, filled with an undercurrent of sex. Before entering this room, she would have found that idea silly, but here, with the energy humming against her, she couldn't deny the sensual appeal of so many people enjoying themselves carnally.

"Get the girl a shot," a smooth male voice said from somewhere to her left.

Anya turned and stared at the good-looking, dark-haired man in an impeccable brown suit.

Sunny laughed and put her hands on her hips. "Master Isaac, I think that's against the rules."

He gave Sunny a devastating grin. "You ladies and your rules. Look, I'm a member of the board now, and I'm making the executive decisions. She needs a shot."

Sunny frowned at him, and the man fingered a small gold pin on his lapel. The other woman laughed and threw up her hands. "Fine! If we get in trouble, it'll be your ass getting paddled, not mine."

Master Isaac grinned and looked over at Anya. "What's

your name?"

"An— Dove." She cleared her throat and tried to keep her eyes on him, not the man squatting naked next to a chair farther off in the room. Using a trick she'd learned from spending her time as a theater seamstress, she lowered her voice an octave, which made her focus on keeping her voice steady instead of on the rest of the world. It worked when she was freaking out about the audience looking at her during her public-speaking class in college, and it helped now. "Dove, Sir."

Sunny raised her eyebrows but didn't say anything about the sudden onset of Anya's phone-sex voice. "So what'll it be, Dove?"

"Do you have brandy?"

Master Isaac smiled. "Girl after my own heart. Get her a shot of Le Voyage de Delamain."

"Would you like one as well, Sir?"

He glanced at his watch. "No, I drove tonight." He gave Anya such a charming smile that she almost sighed. "Send Dove by my table with a bottle of Bollinger and two steins of Utopias in a bit. I don't want the Mistresses convincing her the only way to please a man is to spank him."

Sunny finished pouring Anya's drink with a practiced twist of her wrist. "Are Master Hawk and Master Jesse here with you tonight, Sir?"

Master Isaac shook his head. "Not yet, but they should be here soon."

Anya startled at the name Jesse, her thoughts going immediately to her devastatingly rugged and handsome boss, Jesse Shaw. CEO of a technology company, wonderful father to two little boys, unbelievably sexy, and utterly oblivious of her as a woman. To her dismay, she'd developed a hell of a crush on him despite the fact that he saw her as nothing more than a kid. He'd been a widower for five years after his wife passed away during childbirth. Anya had been working for him for around two months now and adored his twin little boys. They were a handful, as any young boys are, but they were so sweet-natured that it warmed her heart to be near them. Even more, she adored their father to the point of being embarrassing.

Shaking the unwanted image of Jesse smiling at her from her thoughts, she took the shot glass and lifted. "Thank you, Sir, er, Master Isaac. You have no idea how much I need this."

Then she swallowed the drink and moaned in appreciation at the wonderful taste of the brandy. If she'd known it would be this good, she would have sipped it. After work tonight she'd have to find out the name of this brandy so she could buy a bottle.

He smiled and waved, leaving her with a bemused Sunny. "That was Master Isaac. He's superhot, supernice, and supertaken. His fiancée, Kitten, is here with him. You'll like her. She's a regular person like us but now with a five-carat engagement ring."

"Wow." The alcohol burned in her belly, warming her from the inside out.

"Love that sexy voice you did. If I were you, I'd use it all the time here."

Anya flushed and started to raise her hand to twirl her now carefully curled hair, then jerked it back down to her side. "I do it sometimes when I'm nervous. It's a trick to help me speak in uncomfortable situations. I used to be terribly shy, and my mom got me into acting classes to help me gain some courage." She took a deep breath and gave Sunny a hesitant look. "Do you think that's kind of weird? Speaking like I'm someone else?"

"Listen, the minute you walk through the door, you become Dove, sex kitten extraordinaire. Like how I become Sunny, greatest cock tease east of the Mississippi." Both women laughed, and Sunny rested her hip against the counter. "Besides, with your looks combined with that Marilyn Monroe voice, you'll make tons of money."

"Well, I can't argue with that." Anya lowered her voice and grinned before fluttering her lashes. "Hello, what can I get for you today, Master?"

"Fantastic. Now let's get down to business."

———✦———

Anya talked with Sunny about the different kinds of drinks Wicked offered as well as nibbles that could be ordered from the kitchen. Thankfully Anya had studied the material provided during her orientation and could remember most of the drinks and food without having to double-check the bar menu. There was a restaurant portion of the club where members could dine for the evening, but on weekends, most members preferred to play in the club and eat at home.

By the time Sunny had the drinks for Master Isaac's party loaded onto a tray, Anya was feeling a little more comfortable with the surroundings. The Hall of Mirrors bar, as this section of the club was known, was divided up into six sections. Anya and Sunny handled their area while other bartender/server teams handled the other five sections. The room they were in seemed massive to Anya; Sunny had told her that inside the private areas of Wicked, where the real kinky stuff happened, there were bars that were triple the size of The Hall of Mirrors. The server/bartender teams who worked in the private sections of the club were all veteran employees at Wicked. Each bar had its own theme, and the employees that worked there were expected to know exactly how they should behave. For example, in a high protocol bar there were all types of social nuances that the server was expected to know, while in the pet play area, it was considered the norm to serve the submissives there out of silver bowls on the floor. It seemed weird to Anya that anyone would want to be treated like a dog, but that's what some people liked.

Anya had learned to unfocus her gaze when naked people strolled by, looking at a spot over their shoulder. Fortunately the naked people were almost always submissives, so she usually dealt with their Master or Mistress. And sure enough Mr. Florentine had been right about the compliments. Every group she'd served had something nice to say about her appearance. While she couldn't stop her blush, saying thank you instead of stammering out some reason why she wasn't pretty was getting easier by the minute.

Sunny finished pouring the last beer and set it on the tray. "There you go. Master Isaac is toward the back of the room, on the left. Kitten, his fiancée, is wearing a gold cat mask, so that should help you find them. If you can't spot them, you should for sure be able to spot Master Hawk. He's the Native American man with the yummy long black hair held back by a silver clip."

Another one of the servers came up, a stunning woman with hair like ebony silk that reached all the way to her buttocks, and beautiful dark honey-brown skin. She wore a flowing gown that exposed her perfect body and a green mask that made her emerald eyes almost glow. She was stunning, probably the loveliest woman Anya had ever seen in person, even with a mask obscuring half her face, but the look she gave Anya was far from friendly.

"Why are you sending her into my section?" She jabbed her red-painted nail in Anya's direction.

Sunny narrowed her eyes, and her tone turned chilly. "Look, Goddess, Master Isaac requested her. You know the rules. Doesn't matter whose section they sit in if they request a server."

Goddess turned on Anya and looked down her nose at her. "Fine, but keep your hands off the guy with the long hair. Master Hawk is mine."

"What? I have no idea what you're talking about."

Sunny snorted, anger tightening the fine muscles around her eyes. "Goddess is under the delusion that since Master Hawk briefly played with her a few months ago, he's her Master now. Funny since Master Hawk barely remembers her."

"I may not wear his collar yet, but neither do you." The other woman stepped closer, invading Sunny's space as much as she could with the bar between them.

"You had better back the fuck off before I slap the bitch out of you," Sunny growled back in a menacing tone totally at odds with her demeanor up to this point. Anya stared at her.

Goddess leaned over the counter, her nose almost touching Sunny's. The two women radiated enough hostility that Anya was afraid they were about to fight. The air crackled with tension, and she noticed the bartender nearest to Sunny, Onyx, coming over with a stern expression on her face. While most of the bartenders were submissives, Mistress Onyx was not, and Anya didn't want to be in her way when she reached the two quarreling women. Already fire flashed in the Domme's dark eyes, and an almost visible wave of command emanated from her.

Only an idiot would stick around for the fireworks about to go down, so Anya tugged the tray out from between Goddess and Sunny, grunting beneath its weight. "I'll just take this over to them so Master Isaac doesn't get mad at me."

The two women ignored her, and Sunny said in a low voice, "He may have fucked you, but obviously whatever you had to offer, he doesn't want seconds on."

"You white-trash cunt!" Goddess gripped the edges of the counter hard enough to turn her knuckles white.

Mistress Onyx smacked her hand down on the bar, loud enough so it drew the attention of Sunny and Goddess. "Dove, go take that to the Masters. I'll deal with these...ladies."

Anya turned and moved away, not wanting to get caught up in the drama. Really she shouldn't be surprised. If this wasn't an atmosphere ripe for jealousy, she didn't know what was. Still, she was relieved when she glanced over her shoulder and saw Goddess storming away from a now contrite Sunny and an imposing Mistress Onyx.

Moving carefully through the increasing crowd, Anya made her way to the back of the room and quickly spotted Master Isaac. He was seated across from two men sprawled out over the opposite couch, one with long, dark hair held back in a clip and the other with short, deep auburn hair. Next to Master

Isaac sat a beautiful woman with a golden cat mask like Sunny had described.

Plastering a smile on her face, she moved around the side of the sofa the men sat on, and said, "Master Isaac, I have your…"

Her words died off in her throat, choking her as she stared at her boss, the father of the children she watched, Jesse.

Dressed in a pair of worn jeans and a brown leather vest that hung open to expose the broad expanse of his chest, he looked amazing. She'd never seen him with his shirt off, and despite her shock, a part of her brain registered that he was as built as she'd dreamed. All big muscles and strong lines. Soft brown hair curled on his chest and trailed down his belly to the bulge of his crotch. The jeans clinging to his thighs were nice and worn, revealing the vague shape of his dick. Ripping her gaze away from his nether regions, she swallowed hard as her attention returned to his face. When their gazes met, she found herself drowning in the deep brown of his eyes. His strong jaw flexed, and she had the inane urge to touch his short, well-kept beard.

Panic froze Anya to the spot, and she waited for him to say something, to recognize her but he continued to stare at her as she stared back at him.

"Dove?" Master Isaac asked. "Are you okay?"

Kitten leaned forward. "Someone grab the tray for her before she drops it."

Master Hawk took the tray from her unfeeling hands and placed it on the table. "Miss? Are you all right?"

Suddenly, Master Isaac laughed. "I see what the problem is. One of Mistress Chrissy's subs is kneeling behind you guys, giving the world a view of the phallus his good Mistress has shoved up his ass."

Master Jesse and Master Hawk turned around to look, then both made a pained sound and turned back. Master Hawk gave a dramatic wince while Master Jesse rubbed his eyes. "I should have known better than to look. My asshole hurts for that poor sub."

Master Isaac stood and turned her to face him before releasing her arms and taking a seat next to his fiancée. "Dove, don't be frightened by the harness the man is wearing. He's a very happy and willing submissive, and I assure you despite the size of the dildo currently inside of him, he is quite all right."

Master Isaac's words rushed in a meaningless stream over her, and she looked back at Jesse. How could Jesse not see who she was? Yeah, she was wearing a mask, but damn, she knew every inch of his face. And yes, this was probably the first time he'd ever seen her hair in anything other than a tightly pinned bun. Little boys and long hair didn't mix well, but how could he not know her? She turned all the way to face him and watched his gaze travel from her breasts, normally covered by loose shirts, to her lips, normally bare of any kind of lipstick, and finally to her eyes.

The sad realization that Jesse really didn't pay any attention to her as anything other than his nanny hurt. She almost wished he would speak up, even though it would mean the end of both her jobs. No way would Jesse let someone who worked here watch over his kids. She should run away right now, make some excuse about being overwhelmed or something.

Too bad her feet refused to move.

Kitten laughed. "Jesse, grab her before she falls over."

Anya almost fled before Jesse could touch her, sure he would recognize her up close, but as soon as his strong arm gently tugged her into his lap, she froze. He tipped her chin up and smiled at her, arranging her so she fit comfortably against him. "You are a nice armful, little one. Are you all right?"

She nodded, unable to speak, caught up in the heat of his body against her, the smell of his expensive cologne. He continued to look down at her, and her breath hitched in her chest when desire began to warm his eyes. Passion flared between them and her whole body came alive. Something about his attention sharpened, and she felt like he was really seeing her this time. His gaze swept down her body with obvious appreciation, pausing on the swell of her breasts, the deep valley of cleavage between them. Beneath her bottom, his cock began to harden, and she didn't know if she should cheer or scream. This was Jesse, her boss, the unapproachable man who barely registered her existence. The man she'd dreamed and fantasized about from the moment she'd met him.

Unable to form a coherent thought in response to his question, she nodded again and hoped he would let her go but prayed he wouldn't.

He glanced over his shoulder again and gave an exaggerated wince, the move shifting his now very hard and long erection against her. "I can see why you'd be a little shocked. It appears as if Mistress Chrissy put a telephone pole up the poor guy's ass."

She blinked at him, unable to tear her gaze away. Any second now he'd figure out who she was, and she'd be fired from this job or her position as a nanny or both. Anxiety twisted her stomach into tight knots, and nausea filled her. Despite her discomfort, she couldn't help the tiny surge of joy at being held in his arms, admired by him, turning him on.

He cupped her face with his free hand and stroked his thumb across her lips. "Do you have a name?"

She took a quick breath. Her overstretched nerves couldn't get any tighter, so she began to tremble. "Dove."

"Dove." He stroked her cheek behind the mask, his touch lighting a fire between the cradle of her thighs. "Lovely name, and it suits you. Now, Dove, I want you to breathe with me. Keep your eyes on my face and ignore everything else."

That wasn't hard to do, considering for her he was the only person in the room at the moment.

"Deep breath in, hold it, and now out."

His low, whiskey-rough voice washed over her. It reminded her of when he would work with a new horse at the stables on his property. She'd watched him in secret, playing with the boys in the garden near the pastures and drooling over him as he coaxed a young gelding to do his bidding.

"Such a good girl. Keep breathing with me. Relax and let me hold you. You're safe here. Nothing is going to hurt you while you're in my arms. Now breathe."

They did that a few more times, and slowly her heartbeat returned to a somewhat normal rhythm. She was still as stiff as a board on his lap, but with every passing second, her hopes rose that he didn't know who she was. When he looked at her like this, she didn't want to tell him the truth, wanted a few more minutes of being the focus of his attention. The feeling of him, the scent of him was intoxicating. If she wasn't careful, she'd never want to leave his embrace, and that could only lead to disaster.

Keeping her voice disguised, she tried to move off him. "I'm okay, Sir. You can let me go now. I'm probably squishing you."

Master Isaac and Master Hawk both laughed while Jesse grinned down at her. "The day I'm squished by a little thing like you is the day I need to hang up my spurs." He tightened his hold on her and whispered in her ear. "Besides, I enjoy holding you, and if you don't object, I'd like to do it for a few more minutes."

Unsure if he really meant it or he was saying that because he felt bad for her, she attempted to get up again. "Really, you don't have to—"

His grip tightened again, this time holding her firmly in place against the hard lines of his body. Her desire surged, and her empty sex contracted. She tried an experimental wiggle, but he didn't budge an inch. Staring up into his eyes, she relaxed against him, accepting his hold on her. Truth be told there was nowhere she'd rather be than in his arms.

"There, that's a good girl." He brushed his hand along her neck, stroking the delicate skin with his rough fingertips. Jesse still had the work-roughened hands of a man who grew up working on his grandparents' ranch, and she shivered beneath his caresses. Keeping his touch gentle, arousing, and teasing at the same time, he watched her closely. "Have you ever been anywhere like this before, Dove?"

She shook her head, dimly aware of the two Masters and Kitten having a conversation while they sipped the drinks she'd brought them. "No, Sir."

"Hmm." The sound was a deep bass rumble that vibrated her bones. "Have you ever experimented with BDSM?"

"No, Sir." She flushed and thought about the time she'd let one of her ex-boyfriends spank her, but it had been more embarrassing than arousing.

His hand curled around her throat, effectively holding her like a gentle collar. "Now, now. It's not a good idea to lie to a Master." She blinked up at him in confusion. "Your blush gives you away, Dove. So why don't you tell me what you've done."

Mortification chased back her stupefied arousal. "That really isn't any of your business, Sir."

"So polite, even when telling me to piss off." He smiled, his straight white teeth shining against his faded tan. "You are a shy little thing, aren't you? But so pretty, and you fit against me just right. The things I could do to you..."

Unable to stop her foolish mouth, she asked in a breathy voice, "What kind of things?"

"Wicked things."

"Oh." Moisture flooded the cleft between her thighs as her imagination ran wild with the dark, sensual promise of his words.

Master Hawk laughed. "Stop tormenting the poor girl."

Kitten reached out and lightly kicked Jesse's leg. "Great first impression, psycho."

Jesse laughed, breaking the intense mood between them, and finally let her scoot off his lap. "Fine, fine." Before she could fully escape, he grabbed her hand and raised it gently to his lips, the hair of his beard brushing her skin in a pleasant manner. It was as soft as she'd imagined. "Dove, if you ever have any questions or you want to try something out, let me know. In fact, I'll be staying later than usual tonight. Come find me when you're done. No pressure. I'd just like to talk with you."

"I'll think about it, Sir."

With that she turned and fled their section, absently noting there was indeed a male submissive nearby with what looked like a tree-trunk-sized dildo held deep in his ass by some type of harness.

CHAPTER THREE

J esse sat at the end of the bar, watching the new server glide around the room. The end of her shift should be coming up soon, and he wanted to be the first to approach her. Already he could see he would have competition for her favors. Bryan, a sadist and skilled Dom, was blatantly flirting with her while she brought him his fourth water of the night. Jesse worried she might be attracted to the handsome Brit who always reminded him of the devil with his goatee and dark looks, but she didn't seem to be comfortable around the other Master. Right now Bryan was trying to get her to come closer, but she slipped away with a smile. As soon as her back was to Bryan, she let out a silent sigh.

Jesse had always had a thing for blondes, and with Dove's long golden hair hanging down almost to her well-rounded butt, she more than fulfilled that particular taste. Actually, she possessed all the physical qualities he was attracted to in a woman. Nice and pleasantly plump with generous curves, wide blue-gray eyes, and fair skin that easily showed her flush. The sensual epitome of the farmer's daughter. While he couldn't see all her features behind the mask, what he did see attracted him. She was a bit shorter than the women he usually played with, but that only made her even more cuddly and feminine.

Dove reached the bar and leaned over, speaking with Sunny. Her height put her large breasts resting on the countertop, and his palms itched to touch them, bind them in ropes, and make her undoubtedly pink nipples red. The two women laughed, and Sunny looked down the bar at him, clearly meeting his eyes before quickly looking away and whispering to Dove. The curvy little sub stiffened and casually turned her head, pretending to itch her chin on her shoulder while no doubt looking at him. He caught her gaze. A crimson flush spread from her upper chest to her face before she looked back at Sunny.

He didn't think the unusually strong attraction he felt was one-sided. As he'd been watching her, she'd also been watching him. Every time she looked at him, something tightened deep in his gut and a sense of recognition teased his mind. He couldn't think of who she reminded him of other than Marilyn Monroe with her sexy, soft voice. God, he loved a woman with meat on her bones, loved generous thighs to wrap around his hips, a rounded body to thrust into. His dick ached to the beat of his heart, but he was between submissives right now and had no urge to be with any of the willing women available to him.

He wanted Dove.

She glanced at him again, then went back to talking to Sunny. Behind her, he watched Bryan stroll up, an arrogant smile curving his lips. His dark eyes were focused on Dove's ass, and he was fingering the whip he kept coiled at his side. The thought of anyone but himself touching Dove sent a surprisingly strong possessive streak through Jesse.

Before Jesse was even conscious of making the decision to move, he found himself at Dove's side. "Hey, beautiful."

She looked up at him, her pulse visibly hammering in her throat. "Hello, Jes— I mean, Master Jesse."

Bryan scowled at him and stood on her other side. "Hello, Dove. Are you ready for me to show you around Wicked?"

Dove looked between the men, then back to Sunny. The other woman smiled at Bryan. "I'm sorry, Master Bryan, but Dove has already agreed to spend some time with Master Jesse tonight."

Bryan frowned at the bartender. "I don't recall asking your opinion."

The way Dove got offended on behalf of her friend made Jesse fight to keep from laughing. Poor Bryan. He was a stickler for manners and that included submissives not speaking unless spoken to first. Probably had something to do with the fact he was minor British royalty. Either way, Bryan's usual arrogance worked in Jesse's favor tonight.

Dove stiffened, and she took a visible step closer to Jesse. "I'm sorry, Sir, but I did promise Master Jesse I would speak with him. I do thank you for your offer, but my time is already spoken for."

Jesse was pretty sure that was the politest *fuck off* he'd ever heard. Bryan must have agreed, because his scowl turned into his trademark wicked smile. "But of course. I appreciate a submissive with good manners. When Master Jesse is done boring you, feel free to look me up."

Jesse laughed and swept Dove up into his arms, his cock punching against his fly in appreciation at how good she felt against him. "Why don't you go find one of your pain sluts to play with? This little Dove is spoken for."

She squirmed against his hold but didn't say anything. Ignoring Sunny's giggle and Bryan's muttered threats, he carried her across the room toward the base of the stairs leading up to the second level with the private playrooms. A few eyebrows were raised his way, but when he passed Hawk and Isaac, they both gave him a thumbs-up while Kitten shook her head. No doubt he'd hear about being a Neanderthal from her in the future.

Dove struggled more violently against him when he reached an elaborate staircase and took the first step. "Please. Please put me down."

He paused and looked down at her, trying to assess what was making her freak out. "Scout's honor, I'm only taking you upstairs to talk, Dove. I won't force you to do anything you don't want. I know it's hard for you to trust me, but give me a chance."

She shook her head. "No, I trust you. I don't like being carried. Please put me down."

"Fair enough, but if you were my sub, I'd carry you everywhere. You feel good in my arms." He gently set her down, and the heavy weight of her breasts dragged across him in a ball-tightening sensation.

She placed her hand on his arm and looked up at him. "You aren't mad at me, are you?"

He smiled and ran his knuckles over her upper chest, which flushed on cue. "No, Dove, I'm not mad at you. It takes a lot more than a woman asking to walk to irritate me. Besides, right now we're just a Dominant and a submissive. While I expect you to mind your manners around me, I don't have the right to make demands on you...yet. If you choose to spend some time with me and things progress to a more serious level, we'll talk about what I expect from a submissive."

"Oh, okay." She took a deep breath and kept her gaze on his chest. "I'd like to spend some time with you, Sir."

Her voice broke on the last word, and his heart warmed. So nervous and scared, but trusting him anyway. God, how he wanted to put her on her knees right here on the stairs and show her what he could do for her. "And I'd like to spend some time with you as well. Come on. I've booked one of the tamer rooms for us. It's actually a room I had a hand in designing."

He held out his hand, and she hesitantly took it, her small fingers wrapping around his. Trying to keep his pace sedate, he led them up the stairs and to the left, passing a dozen rooms before they reached their destination. The plaque on the door simply read The Cloud. He paused so she could examine it, then opened up the door.

They entered a small foyer with another closed door leading to the room. He leaned against the wall before beginning to remove his boots. "Shoes off. The walls and floor of the room are made up of a special fiber-optic weave matched with some—" He stopped himself, remembering the technology that made the room was fascinating to him but made most people's eyes glaze over when he tried to explain it. "Long story short, the floor and walls are too delicate for shoes."

She did as he asked, her petite feet drawing his attention. Her toenails were painted a pretty pink, and he wondered if she liked having her feet played with. After she set her small shoes next to his boots, she looked up at him expectantly, the blue-gray coming through in her lovely eyes.

"Ladies first."

She gave him a curious glance but moved across the foyer and opened the door.

Her delighted giggle lit a place inside of his heart that had been dark for too long.

"Oh my goodness." She started to take a step forward and hesitated. "I'm sorry, Sir. May I go in?"

He grinned and placed a hand on her lower back, the warmth of her skin through the sheer material burning into his hand. "Be my guest."

She wandered into the massive curved room, her gaze going from the state-of-the-art high-definition screens showing an endless sunset to the massive bed shaped to look like a fluffy cloud. The walls had been angled to further the illusion of being in the sky, and a light mist came from somewhere in the floor, creating a drifting fog.

Restraints were hidden among the pillows on the bed, but the overall effect of the room was meant to be soothing. He wanted her relaxed, and if he was honest with himself, he also wanted to show off a bit. Watching people enjoy his creations never failed to make him feel good.

She held out her arms and twirled, the short dress she wore swirling around her plump thighs in a distracting manner. "This is amazing. It's like I'm flying through the clouds on a magic carpet."

He came in and shut the door behind him. While he watched her, she wandered around the room, clearly entranced by the slowly drifting sunset. She gave him a delighted smile.

"Will the sun eventually set?"

"Yep. It will become full night in here. Just you, me, and the stars."

"Oh." Suddenly shy, she wandered to the center of the room, where the bed rose up out of the fog.

Moving slowly, reminding himself she was as green as could be, he brushed past her and sat at the back of the bed, the special covering puffing up around him like a silky white cloud. "Have a seat." She gave him a dubious look, and he grinned. "I promise I'll stay on my side of the cloud."

Not looking at him, she sat on the very edge of the bed and startled. "Wow, what is this? Some kind of gel mattress?"

"I have no idea. Truth be told, I let the staff of Wicked worry about the details, and enjoy the results."

"Hmm." She settled more firmly onto the bed.

"Now, do you have any questions for me?"

Seconds ticked by, and she opened and closed her mouth several times before finally asking, "Why do you like BDSM?"

Her question took him by surprise. He thought she'd ask something about the lifestyle or what she'd seen tonight, not about him. "If we're going to be discussing my sex life, I want something in return."

"What?"

That one word held so much suspicion he had to fight a laugh. "I want you to sit next to me. I won't touch you, but I do confess you feel mighty nice snuggled against me."

"You think I feel good?"

"Darling, you feel more than good. But I won't force you to do anything. If you feel more comfortable over there, so be it."

She frowned and scooted onto the bed so her legs no longer hung over the edge. "Can't you order me to do it?"

"No, you're not my submissive. All we're doing right now is talking. If something more develops, and I'm really hoping it will, we'll go from there. But for right now, we're two people talking."

"I don't usually talk to people in a negligee," she muttered softly under her breath.

"Me neither."

She laughed and started to crawl over the bed toward him, her large breasts swaying with her every move in a way that made him grit his teeth. He usually had more self-control than this. What was it about this slip of a girl that threw him into a state of rut?

When she came close enough that he could smell her floral perfume, she hesitated. "Master Jesse?"

"Yes?"

"Do you mind holding me like you did earlier?"

The slight tremble in her voice warmed him. So nervous but still craving his touch. She was a treasure. "Come here."

She willingly clambered onto his lap and snuggled against him, her body relaxing in a way that stroked his Dominant ego. "Thank you."

"My pleasure, Dove. You asked me what I liked about BDSM; this is one of those things."

Her wide eyes blinked up at him in confusion. "What do you mean?"

"It's not only the amazing sex that I like. It's also the feeling I get from being with a woman who trusts me to give her the most pleasure possible. I like it when a woman surrenders to me, lets me run the show." He shrugged and shifted slightly so his aching cock fit against the plush curve of her bottom. "It turns me on to turn you on."

Around them the sun set and the sky began to ease into twilight. Her lips softened, and she licked the lower one with the tip of her pink tongue. "I've never done anything like this before. I mean nothing this...intense."

"I know. Don't be afraid."

She shifted and reached up to touch his face with her free hand. "May I?"

"Honey, you can touch anything on me you want."

To his surprise she closed her eyes as her fingertips ghosted over his face, tracing the line of his jaw, the short fringe of his beard, and finally his lips. The gentle stroke of her hand aroused him more than full-on sex with some women had. Now it was his turn to swallow hard. He'd almost forgotten what it was like to have a woman touch him like she cared. The submissives he'd been with since his wife died had been fun but nothing serious. With one caress, Dove went from something fun to something serious in his mind.

Turning into her hand, he placed a gentle kiss on the inside of her wrist. Originally he'd planned to bring her back here and talk. Okay, maybe a little bit of playing, but just enough to whet her appetite for more. Her gentleness woke a territorial beast who eyed the delectable woman with interest. She wasn't like the others; she was more real somehow. Her responses were untutored and honest, sidestepping the careful rules he'd put in place in order to keep his distance when he played with other submissives.

He had every intention of turning their play rough, to establish some space between them, but she opened her eyes and looked up at him in wonder. "Would you kiss me, please?"

A warm hum buzzed through his spine, burning into his hips and filling his cock with a hard pound. What man could resist such a look? He cupped her face with his hand and raised her up with his arm beneath her back. Her anticipation was almost tangible, and he found himself spiraling up into his Top space, a place where focus on his submissive sharpened and his senses expanded, before their lips even met. At the first brush of his mouth against hers, he groaned, electricity sparking through his nerves and lighting a fire deep in his gut.

At first she was hesitant, carefully brushing her lips against his. Then she became a little bolder, licking along the seam of his lips and making his cock ache to be inside of her, between those pretty lips, deep inside her undoubtedly hot cunt. Soon he had her squirming against him, torturing his dick and driving him to distraction.

"Please," she whispered against his mouth. "More."

He took control of the kiss, plundering her lips, demanding she open her mouth to him. With a soft moan, she did, and at the first stroke of his tongue against hers, she gripped his vest and pulled him closer. Well, while Dove may be meek and gentle in her mannerisms, she was a bit of a demanding handful when aroused. He liked the dichotomy of lady in public and hot slut in the bedroom—a lot. If it made him a sexist pig in some people's minds, big deal. He knew he worshipped his submissives, treated them like goddesses, so what some dumb-ass thought wasn't even a factor. And when he loved a woman, he loved her with all his heart.

Her tongue danced with his, stroking against him in a manner that made him wonder what it would be like to have her pretty lips wrapped around his erection. As if reading his thoughts, she began to suck on his tongue, her wiggles becoming more distracting by the second. The scent of her arousal mixed with her perfume. As the first stars dotted the sky around them, he had to pull himself back. They were moving too quick, skipping some important steps, though he couldn't remember what the fuck they were at the moment.

He tore his mouth away, dazed by such an unexpectedly aggressive response from such a shy girl. Although she didn't look very shy now. Her lips were parted and pink from his kisses, while her hand not curled around his back roamed over his chest, touching him as if she couldn't get enough of him. God, it was so arousing to be with a woman who wanted him as much as Dove did, and after only a kiss.

"Straddle me."

She quickly complied, her legs stretching to accommodate his hips. When she reached for him, he pulled back. "You said you wanted more, and I'm going to give you more, but under my terms. If you agree to play with me, you also agree to surrender your will to me, however temporarily. I will not abuse your trust, though I may abuse you." He gave her a wink to soften his words. "Do you understand?"

She nodded, her blonde curls tumbling over her

shoulders. "Yes, Sir."

Moving slowly, fighting his own urges to fuck, he ran his hands up her arms, taking time to appreciate the silk of her skin. "Show me your breasts."

"What?"

"You heard me. Slip the straps off your shoulders and show me those beautiful breasts. You're my woman right now, and your body belongs to me. I want to see your breasts, so you will show them to me."

He placed his hands on her hips and indulged in a squeeze, loving the give of her body beneath his grip. She looked down at his chest again and reached up with one trembling hand to her shoulder and slid the first strap down. The bodice must have been tight because even when both straps were down, it stayed in place.

Impatient for his treat, he said, "Arms behind your back."

"But—"

He released her hips and gripped her chin, then forced her to meet his gaze. "Arms behind your back. Your choice, Dove. You can either stop questioning me and do what I say, or leave."

Anxiety mixed with his arousal as he watched her debate his words. She searched his face, maybe hoping for some leniency, but he kept his expression cold. If he wanted this woman as a potential submissive, and maybe more, he had to let her know from the beginning how deep his need to dominate ran. And truth be told, he liked it rough. Not every woman could take a hard pounding without hurting, and he didn't want to be with a woman who couldn't take it and enjoy it.

Looking up at him, she silently pleaded with him to stop. Unfortunately for her, that made him want it all the more. He wanted to push her past her inhibitions, to allow her mind to go beyond what society considered right and wrong, to make her fly deep in subspace. Once he had her breasts in his hands or his mouth, he would give her pleasure like she wouldn't believe. But in order for that to happen, she had to trust him, had to follow his rules. Everything he wanted to do to her hinged on her ability to give up control to him.

Getting her to reveal her body was one of the first steps toward her allowing him into her mind and her soul. There wasn't an inch of her, inside or out, that he didn't want to know. He was surprised by the strength of his feelings, but he forced those thoughts to the back of his mind. He'd address them later. Right now establishing this basic trust with Dove was the most important thing.

He released her chin and sat back, waiting for her to make the next move. Biting her lower lip, she reached out and touched his hands before looking up at him. "Can you, would you help me? Please?"

Her voice trembled on the last word, a vulnerability that called on his protective side. "Put your hand over mine, Dove."

She complied, and he steadied her with his other hand against her bottom. Leaning forward, he ran his chin over the soft mounds of her cleavage, growling low in his throat. Her cool floral fragrance intoxicated him. She took in a deep breath and let it out with a rough groan that made his lust surge. He tugged down the top with her hand resting on his releasing one breast, then the other. He leaned back and looked at her, drinking in her tight nipples, as pink and tempting as gumdrops. Leaning over, he blew a hot breath on the tips. They went from soft pink to a deeper mauve, and he had to fight the urge to bite them until they were rose red.

She arched her back to him, a silent invitation he took. Beginning at her neck, he slowly kissed his way down, nipping her delicate skin and earning him more moans. Her hips began to rock against his pelvis, and by the time he reached the outer pink of her nipple, she was making a needy sound low in her throat. Using the edge of his beard, he brushed the tip of her breast. She cried out.

"Sensitive?"

Her pleasure-dazed eyes struggled to focus on him. "Yes."

"Mmm." With his free hand, he held her breast and squeezed it. "I'd like to tie your breasts up with silk rope, force the blood into them, and make them even more sensitive. I bet we could make you orgasm from playing with your nipples."

To prove his point, he took one stiff peak into his mouth and began to suck. With his hand holding her ass, he encouraged her to move against him, making sure to raise his hips to meet her strokes. He switched to her other breast, biting at the tip and relishing her little cries. Her rocking began to speed up. How he would love to fuck her, to ride her until she couldn't walk. His cock ached, and his control began to slip. He was a breath away from jerking aside her panties, pulling down his zipper, and slipping into her heat.

With a low groan, he released her breast and pushed her away until she fell onto the bed on her back.

"Why did you stop? I want more, please."

She was such a delectable treat, her dress pulled up to reveal her silver panties and her luscious breasts trembling with her hard breaths.

"Touch yourself for me, Dove. Show me how you like to come. Let me see that pretty pussy."

With her bell-adorned ankles still around his hips, he was able to hold on to her calves when she tried to pull away. He needed to cool off, but he didn't plan on letting her arousal come down for a long time. While she may have dated some stupid young college boys, all eager to rush to the finish, he had more mature tastes. Experience had taught him the longer he built the arousal, the harder the orgasm. And he wanted to blow her mind.

Once again she gave him that pleading look, and he bit back a growl of need. "Show me your wet cunt, Dove. Now, or get out."

She closed her eyes and hesitantly placed her hand over her panties, softly touching herself. Her strokes were tentative, as if she expected someone to tell her to stop. There was no way he was going to be merciful and allow her to not do something that was bringing both of them pleasure even as it embarrassed her. Besides, he rather liked the combination of her hot blush with the way her hips tilted toward her touch. Her body knew what it wanted; now he just had to get her mind to agree.

"Not good enough. I'd bet the farm that isn't how you touch yourself when you're alone, thinking about a man moving inside of you. What do you think about when you touch your hard clit? Who do you picture suckling that nub until you scream?"

The blush that flooded her chest was a shade shy of crimson. Instead of answering him, she pulled aside the panel of her panties to reveal a very wet, very bare pussy. Not an inch of hair anywhere interrupted his view of her pink flesh or the hard clit poking out from between her swollen lips and begging for his touch. As far as distractions went, it worked pretty well, and he forgot everything but the glistening pink in front of him.

Strengthening his grip on her calves, giving her the feeling of being restrained, he sucked in a deep breath of air when she briefly fought his hold before relaxing against him.

"I think about a man much like yourself touching me," she said in her sexy fucking whisper. "I think about sucking his dick, drinking down his cum, about the weight of his body on top of mine while he takes me." She slowly swirled her finger through the honey gathered at the entrance to her sheath, and rubbed it over her swollen lips. "I think about him taking me, fucking me, forcing me to serve him until he is satisfied. I think about how deep his dick would go inside of me, pushing until it hurt. Until I feel so incredibly full, aching from it." She arched her back and gasped, rubbing harder on her wet cunt.

"Go on." His voice sounded like he'd had a snack of broken glass, but he didn't care. Dove had his total attention.

The tip of her finger grazed her clit, and she moaned. "I want that, to be forced to please him. Secretly we both know

I'm more than willing, but I like the idea of being his slave. Of giving him everything I have. Of being his and only his."

"Baby, that is so what I want."

Unable to resist any longer, he ran one of his hands up her leg, delighting in how smooth her skin was. She tilted her hips up, giving him an even better view of her pink flesh. When his finger grazed her swollen labia, she moaned and twisted, but she removed her hand.

"Nuh-huh. Keep touching yourself. You stop touching, and I stop touching." She gave him that pleading look again that only served to deepen his lust and his desire for her to give up control. "Do it."

Her answering moan made his dick surge, and he struggled to keep himself focused on her pleasure. When her fingers returned to her clit, he pulled her closer so her legs spread wider. Using his thumbs, he parted her labia to look at her secret flesh.

"You are so beautiful. Like a ripe peach. I wonder if you taste as sweet."

"Oh please, Sir."

He would have laughed at the desperation in her words if he wasn't feeling so close to the edge. "Not today, Dove. If you want that pleasure, you'll have to see me after you get off work tomorrow."

"Please, please, please."

He slid his thumbs into her, and she arched with a yell against him, her hips thrusting down onto him. Fuck, she was tight and wet and hot. She would feel so good around his dick. Pressing his thumbs against the floor of her pelvis, he then began to slide them in and out, matching the speed of her fingers now rubbing her clit. Her sheath tensed around him, squeezing down on his invading digits like a fist.

"That's it, honey. Give it to me. Come for your Master."

Two more rubs of her clit and she tensed, her sex swelling and almost sucking on his thumbs, making him grit his teeth as he imagined what it would feel like to have her orgasm with his dick inside of her. Then she was coming hard, her breasts shaking with her contractions as she snapped her hips against his hands, straining his self-control. As it was he had to slip one of his thumbs out and use that hand to hold her pelvis, restraining her as she continued to writhe and moan.

When she'd finally quieted to little whimpers, he withdrew his thumb and sucked her juices off, delighting in the musky taste of her cunt. "Fucking delicious."

She groaned and removed her hand from her pussy. "Oh my God."

With a laugh, he leaned over and drew her back to his lap. "Now, imagine that, but your hands are tied and your legs are bound by silk rope. You can't get away from my touch, can't stop me from playing with you how I want. Your pussy, your body belongs to me."

She buried her hand in his hair and pulled him down, kissing him with enough passion he had a hard time pulling away from her. "Sweetheart, it's getting really late, and I don't want you driving home and falling asleep at the wheel. So though it pains me, literally, to have to put an end to our night, I'm afraid I must."

Her lower lip stuck out in a tempting manner as she pouted, but right now her lips were nowhere near as tempting as her breasts. He could bind them together and oil up his cock, fucking her breasts while she came from the vibrator he'd strap to her hungry little cunt. No. No more thinking about that kind of stuff.

He needed to cool off and get his head in the right space. This wasn't the first submissive he'd ever been with, but sure as shit he was acting like some baby Dom who couldn't wait to wet his wick. He needed to get his A game on and give her a reason to seek him out again.

Placing one more kiss on her lips, he then lifted her off his lap. "Are you working tomorrow?"

She crawled off the bed, her ass wiggling and jiggling in

a way that had him biting his cheek. "Yes, Sir. I work the early shift, so I'll be here at five and work until ten."

Easing off the bed after her, he clasped his hands behind his back to keep from helping her as she slid her top back into place. "If you're willing, I'd like to spend some more time with you tomorrow."

She smiled at him—no, she beamed at him. Her face was filled with such happiness that he couldn't help but return it. "I would really, really like that, Sir."

She closed the distance between them and leaned up on her tiptoes. Even then he had to lower his head so she could reach his lips. In a marked contrast to her earlier kisses, this one was soft and sweet but struck him in an entirely different way. He didn't know if it was her innocence, her youth, or something even more intangible, but he felt protective and possessive of her. While he was more than flattered at the level of trust she'd shown in him tonight and he'd like to think it was because he was awesome, from a practical standpoint, she might be a trusting person by nature. There were those in the BDSM community, just like every other part of the world, that delighted in taking trust like Dove's and twisting it for their own needs.

Normally he'd have done something to turn the kiss sexual, to take the emotions from the act and maintain his distance from the submissive. He didn't want to keep his distance from Dove. Irrational, illogical, but as true as the beat of his heart, he felt a tenderness toward her he hadn't felt with any woman in a long time. Something about them clicked together, like two pieces of a puzzle made to fit. Her fingers continued to explore his face, her delicate touch like a butterfly. He needed to get his head on straight, to regain control of the situation.

Letting this slip of a girl overwhelm him with a touch was inexcusable.

"Just promise me one thing. No matter what happens between us, please don't ever play with Bryan."

She stepped back and wrinkled her nose. "That scary guy downstairs? No thanks. He is too...I don't know, maybe strict for me. He strikes me as the kind of guy who likes those total power exchange relationships I read about. You know, where the sub is always a sub, and he's always the Master. No way could I do that."

Laughing, he gathered her into his arms and gave her another kiss. "I'm glad, because I couldn't do that either. I don't have enough free time."

She reluctantly let go of him and gave him a searching look. "Thank you for tonight. I— Well, let's say you fulfilled a recurring fantasy of mine in more ways than one."

Something passed between them, an electric tingle he hadn't felt with anyone but his wife. He tried to tell himself he knew nothing about this girl, that she was just another server looking for someone to explore with, but damned if he didn't suddenly feel like a goofy teenager. She started to lean up to kiss him again, but he stepped back.

"Woman, you are too damn tempting. Now get that delicious ass of yours out that door before I kidnap you and take you home with me."

The smile fell off her face, and she quickly walked across the room. Everything about her body language showed tension and apprehension. Before she could bolt, he caught up, making sure not to touch her.

"Hey, now. I hope you know I was just kidding."

She blew out a low breath but kept her gaze on her feet. "I know. It's been a long night for me." She opened the door and stepped out into the hall. "I'll see you tomorrow night?"

"You can be sure of it."

CHAPTER FOUR

Anya stared at the dry fountain in front of the converted carriage house that was her home on Jesse's property. A light wind blew against her cheek, and she twisted her hair into a bun, the way she usually wore it while taking care of the boys. Far off in the distance a dog barked somewhere down by the Potomac River. The scene was tranquil, a perfect country afternoon in the early spring. Unfortunately her mind was spinning in an endless cycle of half-formed thoughts and guilt, the same words playing out over and over.

What the hell had she been thinking?

No, guilt didn't even begin to describe how she felt. Ashamed was more like it. She was ashamed of the way she'd gotten caught up in the heady idea that Jesse wanted her. Even now it seemed surreal, like a movie she had watched. She traced her fingers over her chin, feeling the slight roughness from Jesse giving her a beard burn when they kissed.

Goodness, could he kiss. He kissed like a grown man who knew what he was doing. She'd never been kissed by anyone with such skill and, well, domination. He'd taken control of the kiss, thrilling her and making something warm and decadent swim through her body until she was a boneless, aroused heap. She didn't have to worry about when to use her tongue, how hard to touch him, or any of that stuff. She'd simply followed his lead, and boy, had he shown her a trick or two.

But no, it was wrong.

She wouldn't do anything with him tonight. She would spend the evening doing her job, then sneak out. He probably had tons of submissives waiting to serve him. The thought of him looking at another woman like he'd looked at her stroked her entirely the wrong way. If this jealousy brewing in her belly was how Sunny felt about Hawk, Anya could understand Sunny's fight with Goddess. Part of her mind whispered she should quit Wicked, but a louder part screamed at her to look at the piece of paper in her hand.

Another wave of unreality swept over her as she saw the amount she'd earned in one night. One thousand, eight hundred and seventy-four dollars and twenty-eight cents. In one night. That was like insane money. Maybe to the people at Wicked this was chump change—the equivalent of a five-dollar tip—but to her this was a life-changing amount of cash. The dream of spending the summer in Paris was now a tangible thing, something she could see herself affording. Hell, if she made this much a night, she could leave for Paris in a month. She hadn't taken any classes this semester, choosing instead to do a lengthy internship with Laurel.

Oh no, Laurel.

Anya didn't think she'd ever told Laurel any specifics about her day job other than she was a nanny to two adorable kids. She really never talked about Jesse to Laurel because Anya barely saw him. As soon as he came home from work, she left to give him private time with his kids. In the morning he was gone before they'd even woken up, so she spent most mornings getting the boys off to school by herself.

He had a babysitter—his mother, Mrs. Kline—come in on the weekends so she could have a social life. As a result she had the carriage house and its gardens pretty much to herself while Jesse and his family lived in the manor. And it was indeed a manor, built in 1824 by some political guy whose name she'd forgotten. Ten acres of land along with a stately home, carriage house, stables, and small family chapel Jesse actually used.

This was a great job. She couldn't fuck up this job. Then

again she couldn't fuck up her job at Wicked either. So what to do, what to do? She'd been asking herself that question for the past two hours.

The sun burned down on her face, warming her enough that she unzipped her jacket. Well, that was one thing in her favor for hiding who she really was from Jesse. While she worked with the boys, she wore comfortable, loose-fitting clothes. They were two very active children, and she'd be running all over the property with them, trying to expend their nearly boundless energy. It was a pain sometimes, but she wanted Jesse to have the best time with his kids that she could. If it meant wearing them out during the day so when he got home, they were mellow enough to stand still for a hug, then it was worth it.

Tipping her head back, she let the sun burn down through her closed eyelids.

The fact Jesse didn't recognize her at all last night was confirmation enough that he didn't even see her, and when he did, she was just the nanny. Last night, for the first time, he'd really looked at her like a person. Like a desirable woman.

His desirable woman.

Groaning, she shielded her eyes from the light and called herself all kinds of despicable names. But no matter how much she chastised herself, no matter how many times she tried to bring up the fact it was a morally reprehensible thing to do, she wanted both. The only way to do that was to lie, but she'd tell him the truth in four weeks. By then she'd be on her way to Paris, and there wouldn't be any weirdness between them. She'd leave him a letter or something, so she didn't have to face leaving him.

Yeah, she'd go to Paris, become a famous costume designer, and come back with the accolades to make Jesse realize she was a grown woman. So what if he was twelve years her senior? He was a great catch. The kind of guy you wanted to marry. A widower who loved his children, was an honorable man, and a fantastic kisser. The thought of his kiss made desire build and burn low in her belly, and she was glad

Jesse was out with the boys today.

Yep, he was the greatest man in the world, and she was a woman leading a double life. Didn't that woman's TV channel always make cliché movies about women leading secret lives? By day she was an honors student with a promising future in costume design; at night she became Dove, a sexually ravenous nymphomaniac.

An unexpected giggle tickled her throat. Letting the feeling spread, she started to chuckle about the absurdity of her situation, then outright laugh like a loon until her sides hurt. This kind of stuff never happened to her. She was the boring girl who had her nose buried in some fashion magazine. The one all the teachers loved, the girl who helped her widowed dad raise four younger brothers. The one who got a scholarship in fashion that took her all the way to Washington, DC from tiny Bedford, Indiana. Home of the Bedford Caverns and small enough that everyone knew everyone in some way. Yep, the girl her whole town had been proud of was now a lying hussy.

Her shirt brushed her chin, and she touched herself there again, remembering his kiss. She'd never been so brazen around a man before and would have never done the things they'd done in a well-lit room. Especially not with a man who looked like the epitome of a hot cowboy. God, that man had a rock-hard body. There were horses on the property, and he spent a great deal of time taking care of the stables. Oh, he had groundskeepers to do it, but Jesse seemed to like helping out.

He'd promised her he'd show her more tonight, and she was praying that included sex. Though she hadn't seen his erection, from what she'd felt, he was a big boy. She loved men with more length than the average six inches. Not that she was a size queen or anything, but it felt so good to be full almost to the point of pain with a man. Her body agreed, and her pussy began to grow sensitive.

Cursing her hormones, she stood and stretched, trying to decide what to wear tonight. She had a room full of fabric remnants, so she could probably put something together. After checking out what the servers had worn last night, she'd learned that pretty much anything would go as long as it was sexy. She knew her own body well enough to know what flattered her, so she'd spend the afternoon in the carriage house making her outfit for tonight. She only hoped Jesse wouldn't leave around the same time she did.

Thankfully the carriage house and its garage were out of sight of the front of the house, and she had a separate drive. Still, she'd have to be careful. Slamming the door shut on her guilty conscience, she crossed the brick path leading to her home and lost herself in the memory of being in Jesse's arms.

—✦—

Anya slipped on the white ballet flats dusted with iridescent glitter and turned her foot in the light of the dressing room at Wicked. Before she'd left last night, she went to Wicked's in-club mask boutique and purchased two masks, one white and one silver. She wore the white one now. Each of the masks she'd picked flared across her temples, giving the illusion of wings. She wore another baby-doll-style dress, but this one was a semitransparent white. She'd put on a pink G-string underneath where she'd replaced the straps with pearls. The bodice of this dress was completely bare, allowing the pink of her nipples to show through the fabric. Despite her determination not to see Jesse tonight, she'd thought of him the entire time she made it, wondering if he would like it.

"Dove! Earth to Dove."

Sunny leaned over her chair facing an old-fashioned dressing table in the women's locker room. Well, it was more like a spa than a locker room. Anya had never seen lockers made to look like elegant wooden cabinets before. Not to mention the assortment of some of the most beautiful women she'd ever seen. She felt like the lone daisy in a bouquet of roses. Pretty but plain when seen next to the more sophisticated beauty.

At the very least she knew her outfit was just as

beautiful as the other women's. Everyone was dressed to impress in outfits that fit great, except for Sunny. She bought her outfits from catalogs, and none of them fit her tall and slender frame properly. True, not everyone paid attention to sloppy stitches or crinkled lines, but Anya saw it, and it drove her nuts in an OCD way.

"Sunny, I need you to give me your clothes after work tonight."

Arching her brows, Sunny looked down at her tight green latex minidress. "Why do you want my clothes? I mean, I understand why you want me, I'm fabulous, but why the dress?"

"As fabulous as you are, you need a tailor." She stood up from her chair and moved to stand next to Sunny. "See, here and here it can be taken in to flatter your teeny tiny waist and give your hips some...girth. And the way it pooches right here makes you look like you have back fat, which is impossible."

"Ugh, it does look like I have a weird roll on my back." Sunny giggled. "And you're going to give my hips some girth, huh. Well, speaking of girth, I heard Master Jesse was all over you last night."

Swallowing hard, Anya tried to affect a nonchalant expression. "Well, you know, stuff happened."

"Good for you. Master Jesse is quite the catch. He doesn't really play the field much, so I wouldn't worry about him wanting to use you like gum."

"Gum?"

Sunny lowered her voice. "You know, some guys use women like gum. They chew them up and spit them out. I wish it never happened here, but it does."

Anya adjusted her breasts for the maximum cleavage possible. "That won't be a problem. I don't think I'll play with anyone anymore."

"Did Master Jesse do something to scare you?" Sunny took her hand. "Please tell me if he did. You won't be in trouble."

"No, no, nothing like that." She sighed and picked up her body lotion with a hint of glitter in it. "I just— I mean, he seems like the serious type. I'll be leaving for Paris in a month. I don't want to lead the guy on."

"Darling, if things got that serious between you, I'm sure he'd follow you to Paris."

For a moment hope lit her from within; then she remembered the boys and how bad she'd feel for taking their dad away from them. No, the right decision was to stay away. "No, it's complicated."

"But you like him, right?"

Closing her eyes, she nodded. "I really like him. A lot."

"I can't say I understand, but it's your decision to make. I know if I had a man like Master Haw—Jesse, I'd never let him go."

Anya started to ask Sunny about Master Hawk, but Goddess was getting ready not too far away from them. "Thanks. Well, I'm as ready as I'm going to be."

"You look magnificent."

Making their way out to the club, Anya practically bounced on her toes as adrenaline filled her. She tried to tell herself it was because she was interested to see what would be going on at Wicked tonight, but she knew the truth. Her heart was racing at the thought of seeing Jesse again. She needed to get ahold of herself. Maybe he wouldn't come tonight. Or maybe it would be too busy to find a seat in her section. Either one would be a blessing, so why did it hurt to think he might not be here?

As soon as she rounded the corner to the back of the bar, her heart leaped in her chest while her conscience groaned. He was indeed here, and he looked as hot as sin. He wore his usual jeans today, but instead of his vest, he wore a broken-in plaid shirt unbuttoned to show a patch of his chest. A thick brown leather cuff wrapped around one of his wrists, making even his hands look hot. It should be impossible he'd look sexier wearing more clothes than less, but for the love of goodness was he fine.

Sunny bumped her. "Stop gawking."

Whipping her head around fast enough to send her hair flying, she turned to Sunny. "Please tell me that's not my section."

"Sure is."

They traded off with the previous bartender and server, catching up on drink orders. Anya helped Sunny out by pouring the beer, but the other woman did all the mixed drinks. Matching the orders to the digital chart beneath the bar showing each table's number, she was glad to see Jesse hadn't ordered anything. Maybe she could avoid him.

With that in mind, she worked the floor, smiling and chatting with people when they wanted it, wordlessly handing others their drinks when they indicated they didn't want to talk. Like yesterday she received warm compliments that had her practically floating. Then she'd look at Jesse out of the corner of her eye, and her body would drop back to earth at the intensity of his gaze.

She'd made her rounds twice and was on her way back to the bar, preoccupied with remembering the fancy drink order a Master had requested, when she passed too close to Jesse. He grabbed her wrist, and she cursed even as an erotic thrill went through her. God she wanted him, badly.

"Dove, is there a reason you're avoiding me?"

"I'm trying to work, Sir." She attempted to tug her hand away, but he held fast, adding to her arousal.

"And yet I'm sitting in what I believe is your section, and you've never asked once if I wanted anything."

She swallowed, trying to think up something to say to defend her obvious snub, but the best she could come up with was, "Would you care for a drink, Sir?"

"Yes. Bring me a vodka tonic. Sunny will know my preference."

His thumb rubbed against the sensitive skin on her inner

wrist, and she remembered how he'd used his thumbs to fuck her, to make her come, to tear her apart and rebuild her piece by shattered piece. Desire pooled through her limbs, dampening the soft skin between her legs and drawing her nipples to hard points. His gaze drifted down to her chest, and his jaw clenched when he saw her breasts.

Holding her wrist at an angle, he brought her close to him, close enough that her breasts were inches from his face. Once again her world narrowed to him, everything else fading to a meaningless murmur. She hoped, prayed he would take her breast into his mouth, but instead he blew a hot breath across her skin, making her moan and arch against him.

"Well, Dove, attraction doesn't seem to be the problem."

"Please, Sir, I'm... Oh God, I'm working right now. I can't think when you touch me."

With obvious reluctance he released her. "Go. Do your job and fetch my drink."

To her great embarrassment, she'd made it all the way to the bar before she even realized she was moving. It was like her spirit was still with Jesse, wanting to curl around him, make him happy, be and do whatever he wanted. Sunny laughed at her dazed look, and that helped to get her bearings. Anya filled the drink requests and took care of the rest of the floor, once again avoiding Jesse.

When she came back to the bar, no longer able to put off getting him his drink without being obviously rude, she was surprised to find a bowl of the most luscious raspberries on her tray along with Jesse's drink.

"Who do these go to?"

"Master Jesse. They're compliments of the house. Molly will be handling your section to help out while you...serve Master Jesse."

Heat burned her cheeks at the obvious double entendre. "Oh, okay."

Conflicted, aroused, and desperately eager to be back at his side, she took the tray and made her way through the now crowded room toward Jesse. As she watched, a pretty redhead in a sheer robe knelt next to Jesse. The redhead placed her hand on his knee, and Anya's heart hurt. She slowed down, waiting to see what would happen. If Jesse started to play with that other woman, she'd give him his drink and go cry. Jeez, she sounded pathetic even to herself.

Squaring her shoulders, she moved quickly to his table. The redhead was sucking the tip of her finger in a suggestive manner, but the only woman Jesse had eyes for was Anya. And what eyes they were. A dark brown that seared her and made her skin feel tight, sensitive.

Holding his gaze, she said, "Master Jesse, I have your drink."

He glanced down at the woman next to him. "I told you to go."

The other woman gave Dove a nasty look but rose and walked away, her perfect butt swaying.

"Dove, eyes on me." She looked back at him and inwardly groaned at the command in his gaze. He glanced at the tray and back at her face. "Raspberries?"

"Sunny said they were on the house." Even using her fake voice, she sounded breathless. Just being near him created an electric charge in the air, drawing her to yearn for his touch.

Jesse grinned and raised his hand in the direction of the bar. "Excellent. Put the tray down; then come sit on my lap."

His drink almost sloshed over the side as she put the tray on the small circular table before him. He reached out and steadied her, one hand rubbing her hip and the other holding the tray. "Easy, little one. I'm not going to hurt you."

The sadness in his tone made her nerves almost entirely disappear. "Oh no, Sir. I'm not afraid of you. I'm intimidated and overwhelmed and confused, and I want you so desperately." The last bit slipped out, and she slapped her hand over her offending mouth.

Jesse laughed and tugged at her until she was once again

draped across his lap, cuddling close. By the saints he smelled good. Musky, like freshly turned earth and autumn leaves. A very masculine scent that must have been loaded with pheromones, because her mind totally checked out, leaving her body to be controlled by her surging hormones. She traced her fingers along the open collar of his shirt, lightly brushing the hair covering the hard muscle beneath.

"Fuck, woman, the things you do to me." He captured her hand. "Behave or I won't give you any raspberries."

She pouted, and he ran his finger over her lower lip. "My offer still stands, little one. I want to play with you tonight. Do you want to play with me?"

Suddenly and absurdly shy, she hid her face against his chest and nodded.

"No, say it. Look at me and tell me you want to be mine for the evening."

Her heart hammered against her ribs. Raising her gaze to his face, she looked at him, really looked at him, and said the truth. "I've been thinking about you all day, thinking about what happened last night. I'm not used to how intense things are. But I want more."

His lips softened, and he smiled. "Intense isn't always bad."

"No. No, it's not."

He leaned over and plucked a raspberry from the tray. "Hold it between your lips."

She eagerly opened for him, groaning when he traced the fruit over her mouth. Once it was safely in place, he leaned over, and she realized he was going to eat it from her. The moment his lips touched hers, she had her hands buried in his hair, kissing him like she'd been starving for his touch.

And she had been. Once would never be enough.

The sweet and tart fruit burst into her mouth, and he slowly licked against her tongue, his low growl making her pussy throb. She was so wet, so ready for him. The memory of his mouth on her nipples had her squirming as he cupped her breast and squeezed before letting it go.

His hand roamed down her side; then he grabbed her hip and pulled her closer to him, his erection straining against her bottom. The need to come became desperate, a sharp pain and ache to be filled with him. Everything about Jesse turned her on. She'd never imagined she could even feel like this about anyone. Being held by him had to be one of the greatest pleasures in the world. The combination of safety and submission made her reckless with desire. She could be as wild as she wanted, and he wouldn't be offended.

He sucked at her lower lip, then bit, drawing a cry from her.

A man cleared his throat from right next to them. "Jesse, you can't have her out here."

Jesse looked up, and she caught a glimpse of Master Hawk out of the corner of her eye. Jesse returned to kissing her, now working his way across her jaw to the sensitive skin of her neck. The feeling of his lips against her there had her moaning and clutching at him, urging him on. Nothing mattered but his touch.

"Let me say this another way. The lovely sounds your little sub is making is attracting all types of attention. As she isn't wearing anyone's collar—yet—you'd do well to not advertise what a delectable woman she is. Hell, man, I want her, and I don't even like blondes."

Breathing heavily, Jesse backed away but not before nipping her neck hard enough to make her body contract. "You're right, and keep your fucking hands off of her."

Master Hawk laughed and walked away.

She reached up for Jesse, wanting to continue their kiss, the rest of the world be damned. He captured her hands in his. "You're coming with me."

It wouldn't have mattered what she said, because the next thing she knew Jesse had her in his arms and was walking toward the stairs, laughter and ribald remarks about what he should do to her coming from the people they passed. Ignoring them, she nuzzled her lips against his chest until she found the hard bud of his nipple. She bit and sucked at it through the shirt, making Jesse's grip tighten on her to the point of pain.

In a matter of seconds Jesse set her down and opened a door with his membership card before pulling her in after him. She had a brief impression of dark stone walls before she was slammed against the cool surface. Jesse pressed himself closer to her, surrounding her, trapping her, making her submit to his kiss.

It was so unbelievably hot.

She gave a little struggle as if trying to get away, and he increased his hold on her until she was helpless to do anything except kiss him back. His cock pushed into her belly, and she rubbed against him, small circles with her hips that had him pushing back. Their kiss gentled, then became more sensual, deeper. He freed her hands and reached between them to cup her breasts, thumbing her nipples.

Everything burned, from her beard-scuffed chin to her throbbing sex, and she whispered against his lips, "Please, please take me. Please fuck me. Please lick me until I scream. I'll do anything you want, just please make me come."

His breath hissed out, and he bent to suck on her neck. The pain and pleasure of his lips had her clutching at him, holding on to his solid presence before the sensations he invoked in her washed everything away. The strong suction of his mouth made her yearn to have his face between her legs.

Eager to encourage him, she reached between them and ran her palm over the hot steel of his cock trapped behind his jeans. He bucked against her, and she rubbed him with long strokes, loving the little shudder that went through him. He reached down and slipped his finger beneath her panties, his breath coming out in a rush when he slid through her wet folds.

"Oh, little girl, you are so wet for me."

One of his fingers probed her entrance, and she cried out, trying to press down on him, to end the teasing, to make him touch her. Unable to force him, she clung to his shoulders and whimpered. Being denied his touch only made her want it more. Her body seemed to grow extra nerve endings, sensitized to his energy.

He pulled away and gave her pussy a hard pat before backing up. Looking at her, he licked his finger. "You are entirely too tempting. For such a quiet thing, you sure do get aggressive when aroused."

Unable to form a coherent thought, she ran her hands over her breasts and tweaked her nipples. He started to take a step forward and stopped, shaking his head. "Dove, I'm going to tie you up."

"Whatever you want, Master."

He closed his eyes, his nostrils flaring. "Get over onto the table, on your knees."

For the first time she really looked at the room and let out a soft gasp. It was a dungeon in the most traditional sense of the word. A variety of canes and whips were hung from one wall, and a set of shackles and chains from another. A large black leather table, easily as large as a king-size bed, sat in the center of the room, and off to the side was an odd-looking chair.

His fist closed in the back of her hair and pulled, sending delicious tingles through her. "Get on the table, now."

She scrambled to do his bidding, climbing up on the padded surface until she was on all fours. He moved next to the doorway and flicked a couple of switches, changing the lighting until it resembled flickering candles. Her breasts hung heavy beneath her, and when he walked around to her side, he let them fill his hands.

The contact of his rough palms against her sensitive flesh had her arching for him like a cat in heat.

"Not yet, Dove. I'm going to make you wait for it."

She whimpered. "Please, Sir. I ache."

"What's your safe word, Dove?"

"Ivy."

"Ivy, got it. If at any point the pain becomes more than you can bear, or you feel like you're going to have a panic attack, say 'ivy' and we'll stop immediately and talk about what you're feeling. Understood?"

"Yes, Sir."

"Do you have any aversion to being tied up?"

"No." Heck, he could wrap her up like a present for all she cared. As long as he was touching her, deepening the connection between them, she'd do anything he asked.

He leaned over and picked something out from the cabinet beneath the table. "First I'm going to tie you up. Then I'm going to fuck you until you're soaking wet and begging for release. Then I'm going to make you come. Now bring your knees together."

She did as he asked, the pressure of her thighs against her pussy making her squirm. He slapped her ass, and she groaned and wiggled some more.

"I see I have a willful sub on my hands." He began to wind the rope around her lower thighs, just above her knees. The rope must have been made of silk because it glided over her skin. Once her legs were bound, he went to her front and tied her wrists together. As she watched his strong, capable fingers taking away her ability to move, she felt scared yet terribly turned on. It helped that this was Jesse and she trusted him completely.

"Kneel up." He helped her get upright, then ripped the straps of her dress so it fell down to her hips.

Holding her by the ropes binding her wrists, he lowered her back down onto her stomach. Being manhandled like this in any other situation would have pissed her off, but it was nice to enjoy what he was doing to her. Not being able to touch him sucked, so she hoped if she behaved really well, he'd let her explore his body.

Her fingers twitched at the very thought.

His warm breath caressed her shoulder a second before he placed a gentle and tender kiss against her skin. If he'd been rough, she would have been ready for it, but this sensual assault broke down her rational mind further. She stopped paying attention to the rest of the room, focusing only on his mouth traveling over her skin, the slight tickle of his beard, how much bigger he was than her.

"Lift your hips."

She did, and he pulled her dress off the rest of the way, his palms leaving a burning tingle against her skin where he'd touched her. Stroking his hand down her lower back, he reached the crest of her ass and paused.

"I like the pearls." His voice came out low and deep, a voice of command even when he was just commenting on her G-string. "Do you mind if I destroy it?"

She shook her head rapidly back and forth. "No, Sir. I can fix whatever you break."

"Hmm."

He slipped his fingers beneath the pearl strand on one hip and snapped it with a swift jerk. The violence of the gesture underscored how helpless she was. While she couldn't imagine doing this with anyone else, she trusted Jesse and that allowed her to relax...somewhat. She was too filled with sexual tension and need to truly be at ease. Next came the other side, and she shivered at the sensation of the pearls rolling over her skin. They plinked onto the large leather pad, and a few managed to roll off onto the floor. She imagined what she looked like to him, bound and surrounded by pearls. A warm rush of pride coasted through her body, making her smile as Jesse growled out something dirty about wanting to shove himself in her little pink asshole.

He teased the fabric out of the crack of her bottom before leaning down to nip one of her cheeks. "You are one beautiful woman, Dove. Your softness is driving me crazy, making me so hard, so ready to fuck you."

"Oh God, please."

She tried to look over her shoulder at him, but he gently pushed her back down onto the table until her cheek pressed against the leather.

"I want your head down like that, but I'm going to pull you up onto your knees. I want to see all of that hot cunt, everything."

A blush spread across her body, caressing her from the inside out with an almost relaxing sensation. She couldn't fight him. He could do whatever he wanted to her. No worries about what he wanted; he'd make her do it without even having to be asked.

With some help, she managed to get into the position he'd instructed her to take. She didn't understand how he was going to touch her with her legs bound together. Then he pushed her back down and arched her ass up, spreading her open like a flower.

"Tell me what your safe word is, Dove."

She tried to clear her mind of the erotic fog drifting through her thoughts. "Ivy."

"Good girl. Let me remind you again, because this is very important not only for you but for me as well. Abusing you and your trust is the last thing I want to do. If at any time you feel like you can't handle it or something hurts, say it and all play stops. I'll talk with you and see if I can help ease your fears, and if it's something you truly don't like, we won't do it again. This is about your pleasure, Dove. I want to make you fly."

Two big fingers slid through her folds, and she sighed, arching her back farther. He muttered some low curse behind her, and she couldn't help but smile. Even bound and awaiting his will, knowing that he desired her, that her body affected him, was empowering.

He slid his fingers down and grabbed her clit between his knuckles. She lifted her hips, making soft pleading noises. To her surprise he began to rhythmically pull on her clit, stretching her tight and squeezing her bud, then loosening and sliding back. It felt fantastic, so decadent and amazing. All she could do was close her eyes and sink farther into the feelings he drew from her with such ease.

"You are too keyed up. I think you need an orgasm before we get started."

She could only moan in reply when the squeeze and release of her clit sped up and he began to push two fingers into her. Even though her legs were bound, she still managed to move with him, rocking back and forth and rolling her spine. She began to whisper his name, reveling in knowing who he was, delighted to once again be the focus of this incredible man's attention.

Abruptly his fingers moved away, and she cried out, then screamed when his mouth latched around her clit. He ate at her like a starving man, devouring her flesh and hurling her toward the depths of her orgasm. With each lick, each brush of his beard against her thighs, she dived deeper and deeper until she stood at the edge of the abyss.

He did a clever flicking motion and plunged three fingers into her, stretching her. Everything coiled, tensed, and strained inside her. She was fighting her bonds now, trying to get more. Then he hooked his fingers inside her at the same time he bit her clit, and she started to orgasm.

She didn't know if it was the position he'd put her in, the built-up arousal, or the fact it was Jesse, but she came long and hard. He stayed with her the entire time, gentling his mouth and removing his fingers, licking her with broad sweeps of his tongue. No one had ever eased her down from an orgasm like this before, and she moaned in appreciation. She felt so cherished, so cared for.

Finally he pulled back and smoothed her hair off her back. "Better?"

"God, yes. You are fantastic. The best I've ever had."

He gave her ass a light slap and laughed. "Darlin', you ain't seen nothing yet."

CHAPTER FIVE

He could still taste her when he licked his lips. Her arousal glistened on her thighs as she completely relaxed. This was one of the things he loved: the ability to bring a woman total contentment. Unable to resist the smooth expanse of her skin, he rubbed his hand over her bottom and grinned when her very swollen pussy clenched.

"Dove, do your arms hurt?"

"Don't care," came her mumbled reply.

He moved to her front, checked her wrists, and examined her for any damage. She was a bit red, but if he cut her loose now, she'd be fine. Eventually she'd build up enough physical endurance to take being bound for a longer period of time, but right now, she needed to shift around and bring some blood back to her muscles.

Luckily he had a good idea of how to do it.

Taking out the safety scissors from the cubby beneath the table, he then gently cut her hands free, then her legs. She remained in the position he'd put her in, and he couldn't help the pleasure that filled him. Even in her submission she was sweet, attentive. Everything about her called to him, and he couldn't remember a time he'd been this comfortable with a woman since his wife, Carol, had died. In fact, in some ways Dove reminded him of Carol.

That thought made him pause, and he gently stroked his hand over Dove's flank, down her plush thighs, and back up again. While Dove and Carol shared similar coloring with their blonde hair and blue eyes, Carol had been a runway model with a lean frame and mile-long legs. He began to press his thumbs into Dove's calves, working out the tension that had built up there, and was rewarded with her happy sigh. No, the resemblance between the women was on a soul-deep level. Both women seemed to radiate their own inner light, a special beacon that called to him. Just like with Carol, he felt immediately comfortable with Dove, connected even as if they'd known each other before. He had to laugh at the fanciful turn of his thoughts. Next thing he knew he'd be contacting a psychic to find out if he'd known Dove in a previous life.

Dove arched, stretching out with a low moan. "Turn over onto your back. I'm going to work your muscles so you won't be sore tomorrow."

She complied with boneless grace, letting him manipulate her while she kept her eyes closed. A dreamy smile curved her pink lips, and he really wanted to see what she looked like beneath that mask. Even more he wondered what she was like outside of the club. Was she interested in anything more than casual encounters? Had she come to Wicked to enjoy the club scene and that was it? While he didn't think Dove was a casual-sex kind of girl, he really had no idea. For all he knew, she could be planning on playing the field, experimenting with different sexual play and Doms. The thought made his stomach clench, and he swallowed hard.

She opened her eyes and held her arms out to him. "Please kiss me."

Stopping himself before he gave in to her sultry request, he leaned down and brought out a bottle of massage oil after putting the scissors and cut rope away. If he kissed her right now, he wouldn't be able to stop himself from devouring her like a starving wolf with a big, juicy steak. When he stood and looked down at her, his dick pressed against his pants hard enough to ache. She was playing with her nipples, pulling them tight and elongating the tips. Watching her squeeze that bounty changed his plans.

Stepping back, he began to unbutton his shirt. She immediately stopped what she was doing to watch him, but he shook his head. "Keep touching yourself, or I stop."

She returned to her play, but her gaze was on him, devouring him with her desire. The way she looked at him made him feel ten feet tall. He finished removing his shirt and tossed it over to the side. Her pleased murmur made him grin, and when he flipped the button of his jeans open, she bit her lower lip. Unable to resist the lure of her flesh anymore, he stripped out of his pants and closed the distance between them, her gasp making his balls draw up tight.

"Scoot over."

She quickly rolled to her side and moved to the center, her gaze never leaving him. He crawled up after her and snagged the bottle of oil. Without his instruction, she lay back and placed her arms over her head, lacing her fingers together in an artless manner he found charming. She was all pale skin, pink flesh, and golden curls. So beautiful, like the steam rising off a river in winter.

He knelt beside her and batted her hand away when she reached for him. "No, little one. I call the shots, not you. Put your hands back as you had them."

She complied immediately, and he rewarded her by pouring a drizzle of oil over both breasts, watching the sheen slide off her stiff peaks and over the smooth curves. Instead of touching her, he drizzled more oil over her body, concentrating on the perfection of her skin and the way he could almost see the blood rushing through her veins.

Once he had her completely covered with thin lines of oil, he began to massage her thighs. Her immediate groan had him increasing the pressure, making the muscles relax beneath his grip. He wanted her languid and limp with pleasure.

Moving up her body, he ignored her erogenous zones, concentrating instead on sensitizing her to his touch. She still moved and wiggled but not as frantic as before her orgasm. He'd make her return to that stage of intense need, but he wanted her to enjoy a slow rush into desperate arousal. Later they'd play with how many times he could make her orgasm in one night.

After all, there was only one first time.

The sight of her skin beneath his big hands made him realize how small she was compared to him. He could easily hurt her if he wasn't careful...and he didn't want to be careful. As he touched her, he wondered if she could take him all the way. Eight inches was a lot for a short woman like Dove. She'd have to endure pain for his pleasure, and not every woman liked that. He needed her to be aroused to the point where she would endure anything as long as it made her orgasm.

After he'd taken care of her arms, he moved back down to her bare pussy, by far the smoothest place on any woman he'd ever had the privilege of touching. He drizzled some oil directly on the split of her cleft, the tempting trail of grape-seed oil down her slit making her tilt her hips and moan.

"Dove?"

"Mmm, yes?" She opened her eyes and stared at him, practically purring beneath his touch.

He hesitated, not wanting to reach for a condom, not wanting anything between them. That in itself was a warning sign he chose to ignore. The only woman he'd had unprotected sex with had been his wife. He knew he was clean, he knew Dove was clean, and fuck how he craved to be inside of her, skin to skin. He wanted more than sex; he wanted intimacy with her.

But that wasn't his choice to make. "Do you want me to use protection? My health records are on file with Wicked so you know I'm clean, but if you want me to, I have no problem with it."

She spread her legs, tilting her pelvis to him. "I only want you inside me. Please, may I touch you?"

He took a deep breath, memorizing every detail of her body and mask-covered face. A primal satisfaction roared in his gut at the sight of the love bites he'd left on her neck. Poor woman would be wearing high-collared shirts for a few days. Maybe someday she would wear a collar made of his suck marks, a visible statement to everyone that looked at her that she was his. His to cherish and protect. His to take care of and make sure she never wanted for anything.

She cleared her throat, pulling him out of his daydreams.

"Yes, you may touch me."

He'd expected a hesitant touch, maybe a blushing caress. What he didn't except was for her to leap on him. He had to spread his thighs to brace himself in a kneeling stance, absorbing her eager hands while she rubbed her body against his. Her enthusiasm overwhelmed him, and he let his hands fall to his sides, giving her an unimpeded view of his body.

She made wonderful noises while she explored him, the hard length of his cock sliding in the oil on her belly. Soon he too became covered in oil, and their skin slid together, a maddening sensation of wet silk rubbing over him combined with the scent of her musk. Her clever lips found his nipple, and he cupped the back of her head while she worked him, her hands gripping his ass hard enough that he wondered if he'd have her fingerprints there tomorrow.

She started to slide her mouth south, but he stopped her, grabbing a delicious handful of her golden hair and holding her still. "We'll save that for another day."

Taking her down with him, he rolled them onto their side, slinging her leg up over his hip. She was still a little too high to penetrate from this position, so he busied himself with kissing her while inching her toward his aching erection. The closer she got to his dick, the more aggressive she became. Damn, he might have to tie her up for his own safety.

That was fucking awesome.

He could actually feel the heat of her pussy before the tip of his cock brushed her wet folds. He knew from last night how tight she was. He didn't want to hurt her, so he teased her, reaching between them to fist his hand below the head of his cock, only letting the tip penetrate her. She moaned and shuddered against him, tossing her head back and trying to press herself down on him.

"Open your eyes. Look at me."

She struggled to do as he asked, and he pulled away completely. Immediately her big blue-gray eyes opened, and the vulnerability he saw in their depths strengthened his dominant nature. Holding her gaze and gritting his teeth, he began to sink into her. Right away her body clamped down, and he had to fight her, pushing up with his hips while sliding her down his body. Her little fingernails pricked his arm and shoulder, but she managed to keep looking at him.

So many emotions raced through her eyes, and he wished again that damn mask was gone. He was almost all the way in when she shivered against him, and her mouth tightened with pain. While he knew from experience most women didn't enjoy a man bottoming out in them, Dove kept working her hips until her lips relaxed, and her eyes became half-lidded with pleasure. She used his shoulder to push herself down until her oh-so-damn-tight pussy had him in a death grip.

Holy fuck and thank the saints she likes it deep and hard.

On their side like this, sex became incredibly sensual. It had been his initial intention tonight to take her any and every fucking way he could, but now in the face of her obvious affection and desire for him, he wanted to make love. This wasn't just about fucking, the meeting of a physical need. Being with her, looking into her eyes, reading the devotion and pleasure in her touch fed an empty place in his soul. The need to fill her, to make her his, to give her everything she needed roared through his blood.

He shoved in a little bit deeper, making her cry out.

Well, maybe not make love in the traditional sense.

He rolled onto his back, easily taking her with him. She kept his gaze the whole time, her blue-gray eyes blazing as he tilted her hips so her clit was smashed against his pelvic bone.

"Too much?"

She had to swallow hard before she spoke, and even then

her voice was ragged. "No."

"Prove it. Ride me."

She placed her hands on his chest and slid her body up and down with a liquid roll of her hips, making his eyes cross.

Goddamn, she felt good.

He rocked against her, setting a smooth pace and slowing her down when she tried to rush. Her hands kneaded his chest, each stroke burying him in her up to his balls. When she gave that pleasure-pain cry again, he wondered if she might have a tiny bit of masochist in her. She certainly enjoyed forcing her body to take him. And hell if that didn't arouse the dark side of his desire.

Remembering their conversation from yesterday about her wanting to be forced, he let the chain on his lust slip a little bit. "I said fuck me." Reaching up, he grabbed her nipple in a hard pinch, and her cunt tried to suck the cum out of him. "Now do it."

She threw her head back, her hair a blonde halo in the flickering lights. Slicked up and wet all over, she was everything erotic, everything female. Soon she kept him in all the way, grinding against him and making a whimpering noise. He reached between them and began to pull on her clit again.

"Oh, please, Master, please."

He pinched her clit hard, harder still until she bucked against him and screamed, her breasts thrusting toward the ceiling and her pretty gumdrop nipples as hard as rocks. When he released her clit, she went completely still, her thighs locking around him and her pussy clamping down.

"Go over for me, baby."

Then she began to come, and he had to fight with every inch of his willpower not to join her.

Before she was finished, he flipped her over onto her back and began to fuck her in earnest, their bodies sliding together. She turned her head and captured his lips, devouring him while working herself against him in a way that made the seed boil in his balls. She clung to him like she was afraid she'd be taken away. He reached between them and played with her clit, coaxing it back to hardness.

"Next time I'm going to put a clamp on this pretty little nub. Nothing too bad, but it will have a long chain leading to the clamps I'll also put on your breasts. That way, when I fuck you and your breasts shake, it will tug at your clit at the same time."

He held her hands above her head when she reached for him, and began to pound into her mercilessly. A couple of times he bottomed out, but when he did, she'd writhe against him and moan his name. Fuck, the things he could do with her. Images of taking her everywhere and anywhere filled his mind, the last being his bed at home. It had been so long since he'd had a female in his bed. Five years. No one had seemed like they belonged there until now.

She arched beneath him; her breasts pressed to his chest. "Oh, Jesse, you feel so good. Fill me up with your cum. I want to feel you shoot inside of me."

Unable to resist any longer, he gave up his controlled rhythm and let his body dictate his moves, reverting to an almost animalistic state where the only thing that mattered was spending himself in the depths of her body. The burn shot from his spine to his pelvis, and he ground her ass into the table. As the first stream shot from him, he roared, a cleansing fire scouring him from the inside out. He emptied himself for what felt like forever, a deep contentment settling over him.

When he came back to reality, he was once again kissing Dove, long and slow kisses that went perfectly with the sweet submissive beneath him. She had her body wrapped around him as much as she could, and he slid his hands down her back, cupping her ass. When he slowly pulled out, her mouth froze against his, and she let out a soft hiss of pain.

"Are you all right?"

She nodded and blew a warm breath against his skin.

"You're a lot to get used to, Master. But I love it. You make me feel so full, so taken." She placed a kiss on the corner of his lips. "I've never been with someone like you."

"How so?"

She leaned back and twirled her hair. "You are just so...so...wonderful."

Happiness flowed through him, mixing with the relaxation. "Trust me when I say if anyone in the room is wonderful, it's you."

She smiled at him; then something moved through her eyes, and she looked away. "Thank you."

Puzzled by the abrupt turn in her emotions, he pulled her against him. "Do you think maybe I could call you sometime?"

She stiffened. "No."

"No?" He tried to keep his hurt from showing. "Do you have a boyfriend?"

"No. No, no. Nothing like that. It's just, well, I mean, you're you, and I'm me."

"Yes, and that's why I like you."

"You like me?"

"Silly woman, of course I do. I wouldn't put up with your bratty ass if I didn't."

"I'm not bratty."

"Oh yes you are, and willful, but that's okay. I like it. Gives me a reason to spank you."

She wiggled against him. "We haven't done that."

He chuckled. "No, we haven't. I'm not going to push you for your number, but I want you to know the offer is there to take it outside of the club when and if you feel comfortable. I promise you I don't have a torture room set up in my basement. In fact I'm terribly dull."

Instead of laughing she pulled his arms harder around her. "You are an amazing man."

"Well, you can't really base your opinion of me on what you've seen here. Someday, in the far-far-far-far-far-off, distant future, I hope you'll let me take you out to dinner. And then have you for dessert."

She laughed and gently elbowed him. "That was so cheesy."

He grinned and nuzzled her cheek. "By the way, nice hickey."

"What!" She tried to pull away, but he held her close.

"Don't worry. If you wear a high-necked shirt, no one will see."

CHAPTER SIX

Anya tugged her turtleneck higher, glad it was the last day this week she'd have to wear something around her hickey-covered neck. Gosh darn that man. He'd left what amounted to a necklace of love bites all over her. It was like he'd marked her as his property. The thought at once scared and tempted her. She could all too easily see herself spending the rest of her life with Jesse and the boys. Unfortunately she didn't think he'd want anything to do with her once he found out the truth.

During their brief meetings throughout the week he'd not even commented on the glasses she now wore. They were purely decorative, part of her disguise in a weird way, but he'd smiled and chatted as usual, letting her fill him in on the twins' antics as they clambered all over him. While he may have seen her the same, she couldn't look at him without wanting to touch, taste, and surround herself with him. She knew how good he was in bed, and it was driving her nuts to have him right in front of her but unable to touch because of her deception.

She looked down at the mixed drink in her hand, wishing she was mean enough to spit in it. Never in her life had she met anyone she despised as much as Diane, Jesse's late wife's twin sister. A mean, vain, and utterly manipulative woman who used her looks to get what she wanted. She'd been divorced four times and had left each man near broke from her extravagant spending. Newly single again, it was apparent to everyone but Jesse that Diane had her sights set on him as husband number five.

Anya took a deep breath, counting to ten twice before she entered the living room, where Diane sat smoking her fake cigarette. The end of the electric cigarette glowed red as she took another puff of the nicotine-laced vapor, then blew the resulting plume of water vapor into the air through her nose. She reminded Anya of an evil dragon getting ready to feast on innocent villagers.

Across from Diane the boys played with their toys, oblivious to their aunt's presence. Not that it really mattered. From what Anya had seen in the time she'd worked here, Diane really only came to the house to visit one person. She usually arrived right before Jesse came home at least twice a week, oozing insincere love for the boys while trying to cuddle up to him. It made Anya want to snatch her blonde hair out by its black roots.

A rather possessive anger flared through her, pushing aside her usual tolerance for the woman. How could Jesse not see that to Diane the boys were an excuse to get her anorexic, Botoxed ass through the door? Diane never actually did anything with them, just sat in whatever room they happened to be in, usually texting on her phone. In fact, anytime they asked her to play, she sent them to "go bother the nanny." It hurt Anya's heart that Diane could be so unfeeling to Mark and Teddy, but it wasn't her place to say anything.

Anya smiled at the boys as she passed them, their automatic smiles back fortifying her against Diane's evil aura. As usual the woman wore a short dress that showed off her legs, high heels, and enough makeup to keep a department store's beauty counter in business for years. She looked impeccable, urbane, and sophisticated, while Anya looked like someone's chunky kid sister.

Forcing herself to be calm, she handed Diane the gin and tonic she'd been told to fetch. Not asked to get, or even requested, but told to go fetch like she was some trained dog. When she set the glass on the table, Diane didn't even look up from her phone, just picked up the drink and took a sip while staring at the screen.

Dian's upper lip curled. "You didn't put enough gin in. I don't know why Jesse lets such incompetent people work for him."

Before she could stop herself, Anya shot back, "I was hired to be his nanny, not his bartender."

Now Diane did look up, and her cold blue eyes narrowed into slits. "I don't know who you think you are, girl, but one word from me and he'll fire you faster than you can blink."

Unsure of the truth of the other woman's words, and not wanting to get into a confrontation in front of the boys, she swallowed her pride and walked out of the room before she hit the bitch. As soon as she made it to the hallway, she ran into Mrs. Kline, Jesse's mom. A kind and funny woman with a dry sense of humor, she often came during the day to help out around the house when the boys were home.

Mrs. Kline gently gripped her arm and steered her toward the kitchen. "Come on, Anya. If anyone is going to have the pleasure of beating that woman, it's going to be me."

The mental image of the round and pretty older woman booting Diane out of the house helped her control her anger. "She is so...so..."

"Mean?"

"Yes."

Anya's stomach clenched as she remembered all of Diane's snide insults about her weight, her looks, and her lack of sophistication. Oh, Diane never acted like that in front of Jesse, and he had enough to worry about without adding Diane's craziness to the mix, but darn if she didn't wish that woman would go fall down a well somewhere and leave them alone.

They entered the kitchen, Mrs. Kline's domain, and Anya sat at the breakfast bar that separated the cooking area from the dining space. "Pardon me if I'm out of line, but why does Mr. Shaw tolerate it?"

"Please, call him Jesse. When someone says Mr. Shaw, I think they're talking about my late husband."

Anya shrugged, feeling incredibly awkward. Usually she and Mrs. Kline got along great, but now she felt all weird after what had happened with Jesse at Wicked. "I don't know if that would be respectful."

"Pish posh. But back to the original subject." Mrs. Kline returned to chopping up some vegetables for a stew she was making. Silver light bounced off the blade of the expensive knife as she diced an onion. "My son, bless his heart, tends to not really pay attention to what is going on around him."

Thinking of how Jesse was totally oblivious to the fact that she was also Dove, Anya couldn't help but agree. "Yeah, I've kind of noticed that."

Mrs. Kline gave her a sympathetic smile. "I'm not saying he's walking around with his head in the sand, but he tends to miss some things. He was like that when he was a boy as well. Always thinking about some fabulous technological invention and oblivious to the rest of the world. Not that it turned out badly, mind you. Being CEO of your own tech company certainly has its advantages." She sighed and scooped the cut onions into a big pot. "I think part of it is that he isn't a good multitasker. When he focuses on something, he gives it one hundred percent of his attention."

Trying to will visions of the wonderful things Jesse had done to her when she had 100 percent of his attention out of her mind, she nodded. "I understand, and I'm not trying to make trouble, but when the boys get older, I hope she doesn't try to hurt them. Not hit them or anything like that, but Diane seems like the type who enjoys playing games."

"You're preaching to the choir, my dear. I have a feeling once Jesse remarries, things will be different around here."

Anya's heart sank to her stomach. "He's getting married?"

"What? Oh, oh no, not at all. I'm just saying that, in the future, his wife won't have to worry about divided loyalties.

Jesse will always stand by his woman."

Wishing with all her heart it could be her but knowing that was an impossible dream, Anya stood and straightened her bulky shirt. "I better get back in there before she decides to try to suck the youth out of the boys."

Mrs. Kline laughed and waved her knife in Anya's direction. "You don't have to put up with her. Jesse would have *your* back if you decided to tell her to stick it where the sun don't shine."

"Thanks, Mrs. Kline, but I don't want to bring any more stress to his life. He works hard and stretches himself thin trying to be both a businessman and a single father. I admire him and I respect him too much to pick a fight with that woman. It's probably what she wants so she can have some drama to cry about."

With a sigh Jesse's mother turned back to her cooking. "You do what you think is best, but don't underestimate my son. I think I've sheltered him a bit too long from what a snake Diane is. Might be time to pull his blinders off a bit."

Unsure of what to say, Anya left the kitchen and almost ran into Jesse. He was taking off his jacket in the foyer, the strength of his shoulders evident as he moved. When he pulled off his dark gray suit jacket, she bit back a moan at the sight of his ass. All that work in the barn kept a man in shape, and Jesse's rock-hard butt did not disappoint.

He turned and, before she could move, caught her staring. He raised his eyebrows. Her heart skipped a beat, then pounded twice as hard. For a moment their eyes met, and his expression turned from amusement to something different. He closed his eyes and opened them again, but before he could say anything, Diane sailed into the room.

"Jesse, it is so good to have you home. The boys have been running me ragged today, but I do love spending time with them."

Anya used that opportunity to duck back into the kitchen. She practically ran past Mrs. Kline. "Hey, I have an important call I have to make about my job over in Paris. Have a great weekend!"

Feeling like a coward, she dashed across the lawn to the carriage house, sweating her ass off beneath the chunky turtleneck she'd had to wear all week. Thank goodness she'd remembered her fake glasses. Now that she was out of sight of the house, she stopped running and took the glasses off, rubbing the space between her eyes.

Dammit, this was so messed up. Having to lie constantly was really screwing with her sense of self. Before this she'd never lied about anything major. Okay, so she'd lied that time she told her mom she was going to Sarah's house after prom and ended up in a hotel room losing her virginity instead, but that was nothing compared to this. She'd be almost ready to call it off and quit working at Wicked, if not for the memory of the soft brush of Jesse's beard against her lips, the way he held her with such...command. The thought had her body readying for him.

Unable to resist the need to be with Jesse again, she went into her sewing room and put various outfits on her mannequins, trying to figure out what she wanted to wear tonight.

—+—

Jesse tried to keep his temper in check as his former sister-in-law, Carol's fraternal twin sister, Diane, rattled off yet another list of opinions on how to raise the boys. Unfortunately, she was utterly bat shit if she thought he was doing anything she said. While she was the boys' only living relative on their mother's side, Diane had made Carol's life a living hell when they were kids. It made Jesse weary of Diane, because in his experience once a bully, always a bully. Despite the fact he found her beyond irritating to be around, he still made room for her in the boys' life.

"One of my favorite therapists was on Dr. Phil yesterday, and he had so many fascinating things to say about the terrible consequences of attachment parenting."

Nodding along with her words, watching her bleached-blonde head bop around as she talked, he then looked out the window over her shoulder and thought about Dove. Not in a sexual sense—being around Diane was an instant hard-on killer—but more in a fascinated way. She was so passionate, so trusting. He was glad he was her first Dom, because the kind of trust she showed in him was almost scary. If he'd been an unscrupulous man, he could have done a major mind fuck on her. Some assholes loved that, and the only way they got off is if they'd hurt someone emotionally.

His thoughts must have been reflected on his face, because she abruptly stopped speaking and frowned at him. "Are you listening to me?"

"Of course I am. You worry I'm coddling the boys, and I'm not. End of story."

Her lips thinned into an angry line. "You'll never find a wife if you don't romance her, and you can't romance a woman when you spend ninety percent of your free time with your children."

Anger flared within him, and he stood. "Diane, I don't need to go looking for a woman."

Her mood changed, and her gaze softened. "I know. You have all you need right here."

She reached up to touch him, but he backed away before she could, his thoughts already having turned back to Dove. "Right. I'm going to go see if my mom needs help in the kitchen."

Diane's cosmetically enhanced lips curled in distaste. "You do that. I'll stay here and play with the boys." She reached into her purse and pulled out her cell phone.

Jesse quickly walked away, tired of having her in his house. She was so damn annoying. When he'd been married, Diane was never around, but once Carol passed, she was here twice a week, more if he'd let her. When she suggested she should spend the night so the boys would have a motherly presence in the house, he'd drawn the line.

The delicious scent of beef stew filled the air the closer he got to the kitchen. Taking in a deep breath, he let the smell of his mom's cooking heal him from the inside out. His mother had only been nineteen when she'd had him, the young bride of a marine. Then when Jesse was three, his father passed away from a brain aneurysm.

His mother had found herself alone, without an education beyond high school, and a small pension to raise her son on. Instead of giving up, his mother had pulled herself up by her bootstraps. She'd managed to raise him with the help of her parents on their big ranch outside of Dallas, get a degree in business, and open her own successful home business making candles. Then she'd met her second husband, Jesse's football coach, Guy, and had remarried. In a grim coincidence, a year after Carol passed, Guy had a massive heart attack and didn't make it. Jesse had moved his mother east with him so they could both heal together and, truth be told, because he needed her. Now she had her own candle-making business here in DC, and it was doing so well that she was considering opening a second store.

He took a moment to admire her and say a private prayer of thanks for having such a great mother.

"Hi, Mom."

His mother looked up from the stove. "Is Diane still here?"

He nodded, and they both grimaced. His mother moved efficiently through the kitchen, her faded blonde hair up in a bun. She was the kind of woman who only felt alive when she was busy, so he was used to her frenetic energy. She turned her back to him and stirred the pot with a wooden spoon.

Trying to sneak up on her, he snatched a carrot from the stew pot, and his mother smacked his hand with her spoon.

"Get out of there. If you want to eat with us, then you can sit down and be a good example to your boys."

He grinned and kissed her on the cheek. "Aww, you're no

fun."

"Neither are you." She smoothed her hair off her cheek from where it had escaped her bun. "Why don't you go ask Anya if she wants to eat with us?"

"The nanny?"

"Yes, the woman who spends every day taking care of your children. You know, the one your boys adore?"

He rolled his eyes and then glanced at the clock. Dove's shift wouldn't end for another four hours. He had plenty of time to hang out before he had to leave. Might be nice to have Anya join them. Though if his mother was expecting a lively dinner companion, she'd be sorry. Anya was as quiet as a mouse, and getting more than two sentences out of her at a time was a struggle. It would be good to see if he could get her to open up. She was a bright kid with a bright future.

"Mom, it's a Friday night. I'm sure she's out and about doing whatever it is young people do."

His mother laughed. "Oh yes, you are so old and wise at the age of thirty-four. Did you get a senior citizens' discount yet?" She turned to face him, untying the green apron from her waist. "Jesse, you need to get out more. You haven't brought anyone home to meet me since Carol passed away."

"Mom, leave it alone."

"I can't leave it alone. You're my son. Besides, I've been widowed twice in case you've forgotten. And each time I never thought I could love again, but we aren't meant to be alone. We all need somebody to love."

He looked out the window at the back lawn. "You're right."

"Of course I am. Now call that pretty slip of a girl and invite her over. At the very least she can neutralize some of Diane's sour with her sweet."

"Good point. I'll just walk over there. I could use the fresh air, and I need to check on the horses. I don't want her walking alone in the dark either."

"Good to see some of my efforts to instill manners in you has paid off."

He shook his head and walked to the mudroom, grabbing his jacket off the hook before throwing it on and heading out. As he strolled across the vast lawn separating the main house from the carriage house, he wondered how his mom would have reacted if he told her a woman had managed to open the door to his heart but he didn't even know her real name. In fact, he didn't know anything about her other than she worked at Wicked.

That would change tonight. Somehow he was going to get some information out of Dove; he didn't care if it was only an e-mail address. He wanted to know her, wanted to understand why he was so attracted to her. In a weird way, it felt as if he knew her, but he sure as shit would have remembered a woman with a body like that. The memory of her scent filled his nose, and he closed his eyes and paused for a moment in the cold spring air. At that moment it seemed like he could almost feel her. Anticipation coiled in his gut. He couldn't wait to get to Wicked. Maybe he should put a temporary collar on her, something to let the other Doms know he was staking a claim.

The carriage house came into view, a light from inside shining through the French doors, illuminating the patio. He ran his fingertips over the smooth stone surface of the fountain and remembered how delighted Carol had been when they'd found it at an antique auction. For a moment he paused and closed his eyes, sending up a silent thank-you to heaven for their time together.

The wind blew cold against his cheeks, and he pulled his jacket tight. It was easy to forget how chilly spring nights could be. Eager to be inside, he moved across the patio to the French doors and stopped dead in his tracks. Hot, bitter bile filled his mouth as he stared at Anya's sewing room, at the glittering costumes on the mannequins, at the mask sitting on a small table.

No. It couldn't be possible.

The closer he got to the doors, the more apparent it became that he had a huge problem.

There, displayed on mannequin forms beneath the recessed lighting, were the costumes Dove had worn at Wicked. He stared in disbelief, standing close enough to the glass that his breath fogged the surface. What were Dove's costumes doing here?

Maybe Anya was making the costumes for Dove.

Maybe they were friends.

Maybe he was full of shit and making up excuses for what had been underneath his nose the whole time.

Yeah, two young blonde women who were of a similar height just happened to know each other. He tried to imagine Anya without her baggy clothing, tried to see past the puffy shape they gave her. His heart thudded in his chest, and he couldn't believe how fucking blind he'd been. True, his mind was often on something other than the present, always thinking about the technology they were developing at his company or the boys, but how could he have missed this?

Maybe he was wrong.

Angry, confused, and feeling betrayed, he turned the handle of the door and jerked it open. Walking past the costumes and rolls of fabric, he went into the small living room looking for something. A pair of sneakers were neatly placed next to the door, and he couldn't help but notice how small they were. Anya wasn't very tall and her petite feet matched Dove's. When he spotted the picture of Anya with another girl on the mantel, he grabbed it, staring at her face.

Anya's hair was back like she usually wore it, and she had her head tilted away from the camera, but he studied her profile and knew without a doubt that his nanny was indeed Dove. The strength went out of his legs. He slumped into the padded chair next to the fireplace, his mind spinning. What the fuck was she doing?

How could she possibly have know Wicked even existed? It wasn't like he ever talked about the club with his family, so there was no way she could have overheard him. Did she follow him to Wicked one night? Had she gotten a job at Wicked with the intent to seduce him?

No, that wasn't right. He thought back to their first meeting and her odd reaction. She'd been shaking enough that the sheer fabric of her costume rippled like water. Which drew his gaze to her breasts and then the rest of her body. Fuck, by the time he'd looked up to study her face, half covered by the mask currently sitting on the table in front of him, he'd already been in lust. She'd been so resistant about being comforted, then had melted against him.

At the time he'd written it off as another newbie sub being freaked out by the scene, but now that he thought about it, she hadn't been staring at the room in horror.

She'd been staring at him in shock.

He groaned, then thumped his head against the back of the chair. It also explained her reluctance the next night to be with him. It wasn't because she was scared of what he was going to do with her or that she didn't want him. She'd been trying to avoid him because she knew who he was. And yet that didn't stop her from following him, from being everything he'd ever desired in a woman...a very young, inexperienced woman.

Double fuck.

He had no business being with her. She was just starting her life, while he'd been there and done that. There was no way she'd want to settle down with a man with two children. Not that he wanted her. Fuck, he was so mad at her! How dare she play him like this, make him fall for her, make him want a future with a woman who didn't really exist. She was a liar and a manipulator. In fact he should fire her as soon as she came home.

The instant he thought that, his heart constricted and regret mixed with his anger. Standing, he carefully put the picture back on the mantel and stared at her face. She was beautiful. Without the mask covering her features, she looked like she'd be carded if she tried to buy cigarettes. Beyond all the lies and deceit, he had no business messing with someone as young and inexperienced as Anya.

Things began to click into place. All week she'd been skittish and had talked even less than usual. Shit, that was another thing: her voice. While Dove sounded like smoky sex, Anya had a pleasant but normal voice. He couldn't reconcile the oh-so-fucking sensual Dove with the reliable and sweet Anya. For a brief moment he considered the fanciful notion that Anya had a twin sister, but that lasted all of two seconds.

He should go right now and call Anya on her cell phone and tell her the jig was up, but he couldn't. She hadn't really done anything to hurt him; in fact, she'd given him some of the best nights he'd had in a long time. Still, it would be very wrong to continue with the charade, to indulge himself in her smooth, young body and her boundless passion.

Smacking his forehead with his hand, he tried to clear all the sexual thoughts of Anya out of his mind, to look at it from an objective angle. Maybe if he could earn her trust a little bit more, she'd open up to him. Truth be told, he didn't want to lose her, either as a submissive or the boys' nanny. Yeah, he had a replacement nanny lined up for when Anya left for Paris, but that woman wouldn't start for another month.

The thought of Anya heading overseas, leaving him behind with only memories of their time together, firmed his resolve to get this mess worked out as soon as possible.

He, better than most, knew how precious time was.

CHAPTER SEVEN

Anya only had three more weeks until she left for Paris. Yesterday she'd booked her flights and contacted a real estate agent, trying to find an apartment in Paris she could rent for three months. Even with her newfound wealth, a place in the city would be crazy expensive but worth it.

Speaking of worth it, she looked around for her Master. So far she'd only seen Jesse once tonight. He'd said he had some people he needed to talk with and that he would be waiting for her in the atrium after she got off. At the time she'd been so overwhelmed at seeing him again, it didn't occur to her until too late that she had no idea where the atrium was.

So now she wandered through the massive building, passing through a series of hallways before she had to admit she was lost. They really needed some kind of map around here, one of those big ones with a little red pin that said you are here. There wasn't anyone she could see in either direction, so she decided to backtrack and find someone who could help her.

The sound of women's voices came from somewhere ahead of her, and she followed the sound to a T at the end of the hall. Before she turned the corner, she heard Mistress Onyx's distinct and very deep voice.

"Goddess, you have to stop this."

Anya stepped back, unsure if she should interrupt them. Then the soft sound of crying reached her ears, and she froze.

"Mistress, I'm so fucked up. He broke something inside of me. I can't trust anyone, but I need a Master."

"I understand, and if that child-molesting bastard wasn't already in jail, I'd go hunt him down and kill him."

"I wasn't a child. I was sixteen."

"Baby girl, you weren't old enough to buy cigarettes, and some mind-fucking Dom found you on the Internet and lured you away from your home, then held you captive and made you his slave. He deserves to rot in hell."

Something hit the wall, and Goddess said in an angry whisper, "I don't want to fucking talk about him."

"Okay, okay. But you have to stop getting physical with the Doms. There is only so many times I can step in and keep you out of trouble."

"I'm sorry. Master Vince touched my arm, and he pressed down where it had been broken. For a second my mind like flashed back to when my Ma—that bastard broke it."

Mistress Onyx let out a weary sigh. "I wish we were gay and I could take you on as my submissive. Some submissives can separate their daily lives from the sexual life, but for you, it is one hundred percent. That makes you a very rare commodity in the BDSM world. I just hope someday you'll find someone you can trust, someone who can help you heal. A Master worthy of the gift of your submission."

For a long moment there was quiet, then more soft crying but muffled this time, like someone was holding Goddess.

Moving as quietly as she could, Anya went back the way she'd come and took a different direction. Her mind was filled with the implications of the conversation she'd just overheard, and her heart swelled in sympathy for Goddess. Yeah, Anya had heard some of the horror stories about women being abused, even killed by the predators who lived everywhere in the world. There were bad and good people in BDSM, but also a large pool of potential victims. Submissives who wanted to believe the best in someone, wanted to belong.

She took another corner, barely aware of where she was

going, and almost ran into a small table holding a vase full of orchids. Before she could turn, a pair of big hands slid up her arms, and she jumped, or at least she would have if those hands hadn't clamped down on her firmly.

"Dove, what a pleasant surprise."

With her heart hammering in her ears, she glanced over her shoulder and mentally cursed at the sight of Master Bryan. He wore his usual black leathers and black T-shirt that showed off the powerful build of his arms and chest. With his dark eyes, goatee, and black hair, he had a sinister air about him that his sensual smile didn't help to soften.

"Please let me go. Master Jesse is expecting me."

"Ah yes, Master Jesse. Are you tired of him yet?"

She jerked away from Master Bryan, her arms stinging where his hands had been. "No. Actually I find him fascinating."

Master Bryan took a step toward her, not touching her but invading her space. "Do you know what I find fascinating? Watching the blood rush to a submissive's skin as I cane her, smelling the musk of her arousal while she comes from being paddled. Pale, creamy skin like yours is my favorite. It would show my marks so well."

"Look, Bryan—"

"That's Master Bryan, girl. Though you may be Master Jesse's sub of the moment, I expect you to extend me the courtesy of minding your manners." He fingered the whip at his side, and her body broke out in a stinging sweat. Just the thought of anyone using a whip on her made her ill. "Stop looking at me like that. I'm not going to whip you. I just happen to enjoy irritating your Master, and nothing would bother him more than another Dom touching his property."

"You're scaring me."

He laughed and glanced down at his watch. "If I didn't know better, I would say you're trying to flirt with me. I find a little fear makes a submissive's orgasm all the sharper, sweeter."

She didn't know what to say, frozen by the predatory look in his gaze. "Sir, I need to go find my Master."

"I'm almost tempted to keep you with me, but despite what the submissive gossip says, I never force a woman." Without giving her any warning, he spun her around and gave her a hard slap on the ass that made her yelp. "Off with you. If I catch you before you reach the hallway at the count of fifteen, I'll know that despite your protests, you do want to play."

Stumbling in her haste to get away from him, she tried to ignore his deep voice as he counted. When she reached the end of the hall, she took a left and let out a scream when she ran into something very big hard enough to knock her on her ass.

"Whoa. Easy, lass."

She dragged in a breath. "Sorry."

She scrambled to her feet and caught a quick impression of a bear of a man in black combat boots and what appeared to be a leather kilt. His skin was a beautiful light mocha brown that made his hazel green eyes all the more startling. He had an amused but kind smile that dropped off his face when Master Bryan rounded the corner seconds later. The man in his kilt held his hand out to her, and she gratefully took it, her chest heaving like she'd run a mile instead of the length of a hallway.

Bryan came to an abrupt halt and cocked his head to the side. "Liam," he said with a sneer, his English accent turning the word into something that sounded like a curse. "I do hope you didn't do something to that girl to make her scream."

The big man in the kilt pushed her fully behind him and said in a heavy Scottish accent, "Well, if it isn't the anemic Sassenach. So desperate you have to chase the lasses now?"

Master Bryan drew himself up tall and looked down his nose at Master Liam. "Hardly. Now go fuck some sheep and leave the girl alone."

Master Liam laughed and looked down at Anya. "Is that true, lass? Did you fancy shagging that wee *nyaff?*"

She wasn't sure exactly what he'd said, but she knew

what "shagging" meant. "No, Sir. I was on my way to meet Master Jesse at the atrium, and I got lost."

Master Liam nodded and held out his arm. "Then it would be my pleasure to escort you to your Master."

"He's not her Master...yet," Master Bryan said with a small smile. "Though he'd better collar her quick before someone calls his bluff."

Ignoring Master Bryan, Master Liam tucked her hand under his arm and led her down the hall. She and Master Liam walked in silence. When they reached the huge entrance foyer without incident, she let out the breath she'd been holding, a tremble going through her body.

"Easy now." Master Liam paused and patted her hand. "Don't let that tosser intimidate you."

She cleared her throat, trying to shake off the nasty feeling in her limbs as the adrenaline faded. "Thank you for stepping in. I don't think he was going to hurt me, he said something about wanting to annoy Master Jesse, but he sure does know how to scare a girl."

Master Liam's laughter boomed through the two-story room. People passing by turned to give them an amused look. "That he does. Don't let it get to you. Some submissives adore him, but I think he's a pompous ass."

She giggled but wisely chose not to say anything. After Master Bryan's quip about not minding her manners, she didn't want to give any other Master a reason to be upset with her, especially a big man like Master Liam. His biceps flexed against her hand as they walked, and she couldn't help but notice how good he looked in his kilt. She was Master Jesse's through and through, but only a dead woman wouldn't appreciate the burly Scotsman.

Disconcerted by the growing attraction she felt to the other man, she decided to put some physical distance between them. Master Liam had the same aura of control and power Master Jesse had, but a little bit different. Like dark chocolate instead of milk chocolate. Both were tasty, but she liked milk chocolate the best.

She went to let go of his arm, but he placed his big hand over hers, keeping her in next to him as they strolled across the foyer. There wasn't anything sexual about his touch, so she relaxed and let him guide her through an archway to the left of the main doors. "I'm sorry again that you had to escort me, Sir. I hope I didn't interrupt your evening too much."

"Not at all, lass. My show won't start for another hour."

"Show?"

Ignoring her question, he paused and smiled down at her, his dark green eyes sparkling with a mischief that matched his smile. "Your Master is Jesse with the beard, right?"

"Yes." He gave her bare neck a pointed look, and she flushed, resisting the urge to cover the band of hickeys Jesse had put there like a brand. "Maybe not officially, but he is. I don't want anyone else."

"Good. He's been rather possessive of you, warning off the other Doms and all that. It's nice to see you're as besotted with him as he is with you."

She blinked up at him, delight unfurling through her in a slow, sweet wave. "He's besotted with me?"

Master Liam didn't respond, just led them into a lovely atrium that reminded her of something from a Victorian picture book. Plants grew everywhere out of giant brass pots, and a low hum of conversation filled the air from the people seated at wrought-iron tables beneath the warm lights. The air had a fresh, green smell, and she took a deep breath, searching for her Master.

Jesse must have seen them first, because when she spotted him, he was already on his way over. Her greeting died in her throat when she saw the angry look on his face, and she tried to remove her hand from Master Liam's arm, but he tightened his grip. Jesse wore a pair of dark brown leather pants tonight that clung to his long legs, and her favorite vest, the one that showed off the sectioned muscles of his abdomen as he neared them.

Jesse's voice came out in a low growl. "Liam, what are you doing with my submissive?"

Instead of being offended, Master Liam chuckled. "Easy there, cowboy. Your lass was lost, wandering around the S and M wing."

Jesse paled and looked at her, his whole demeanor changing to concern instead of anger. "Dove, what were you doing over there?"

She was proud her voice didn't shake when she responded. "I didn't know where the atrium was, and I got lost."

Jesse let out a low sigh. "I was worried about you."

Master Liam let go of her hand, and she went immediately into Jesse's arms, closing her eyes and burying her face against his chest. Jesse stroked her hair with a gentle touch. "Thank you for bringing her to me, Master Liam."

"You're lucky I found her. Master Bryan was chasing after her when she ran into me."

Jesse tensed, and his grip tightened to the point where she had a hard time drawing a breath. "I'll kill him."

"Relax. Nothing happened. He may have scared her a bit, but he never laid a finger on her."

Jesse tilted her head up and looked in her eyes. "Is that true?"

Wanting to avoid any confrontation between the two men, she downplayed the incident. "Yes, Sir. He said he was just trying to annoy you, but he still creeped me out."

Both men laughed; then Master Liam shifted next to them, and Jesse turned his attention back to the other man. Jesse put a possessive arm around her waist. "I'm in your debt."

The Scot grinned and rubbed his chin. "That you are. Does your girl fancy a bit of voyeurism? One of the lasses I'm training would love her."

Jesse grinned. "Let me have a moment alone with her. Where are you set up tonight?"

"Over in the London Theater."

"Is Master Rory with you?"

"Nae. He's off dealing with some *eejit* over mineral rights in North Dakota."

Jesse ran his thumb over her shoulder, the touch making her relax further. "If I don't see you again tonight, thank you. It's nice to know I have such good friends."

"Most welcome. I know you'd do the same for me." He gave Anya a wink that had a decidedly carnal edge to it. "Hopefully I'll see you again in a bit."

Master Liam turned, his kilt flaring briefly to reveal his heavily muscled thighs. She watched him walk away, then turned to look up at Jesse. "I'm sorry I caused so much trouble."

Not responding, he led her over to a black wrought-iron bench toward the back of the room. After taking a seat, he pulled her onto his lap and stared intently into her face. His lips moved like he wanted to say something, but he didn't. Worried she'd upset him, she cuddled closer.

"Please don't be mad at me."

He closed his eyes before placing his lips against her head. "What am I going to do with you?"

"Let me make it up to you with a blowjob?"

He laughed and stroked his hand down her side, some of the tension leaving his body. "I've been greedy with your time, keeping you all to myself and not showing you what the club has to offer."

"I don't want anyone else."

He pulled back, his dark brown eyes boring into her. "How do you know? You're so young, and there is a whole world out there to explore. I should let you go so you can experience life without being shackled to an old man."

Disconcerted by the turn in their conversation, she

sought to reassure him and herself. "Please, Master Jesse. Things are so much better when I'm with you, and you're not old. You're wonderful. Plus I don't want to be alone or with anyone else. If there are things you think I should experience, that's fine. I trust your judgment. I want you to be the one who teaches me, who helps me explore. Just please don't leave me."

He ran his thumb over her lower lip. "Easy, little one. I'm not going anywhere." He cleared his throat and smiled. "Have you ever watched anyone have sex?"

Heat flared in her face like someone was roasting her from the inside with a blowtorch. "No."

"Would you like to?"

"I-I don't know. It's not something I ever thought about."

"What about watching Master Liam pleasure his submissive? Be honest with me about your desires, Dove. I will find them out one way or another, and it would be much easier for you if you admitted your dark and dirty secrets."

Now the heat in her cheeks flared to the temperature of the sun. "As long as you're with me, I think I would like it."

He lifted her off his lap and stood. "Follow me."

CHAPTER EIGHT

A short time later they were in a dimly lit room illuminated by flickering gas lanterns hanging from the high ceiling. Anya took a deep breath to brace herself, and the scent of sex and perfume filled her. Sumptuous red-velvet couches surrounded a circular stage that rose a few feet off the floor. Those were almost all occupied, with only a few empty spots at the back of the room. The stage itself was large, with a black leather table, chains hanging down from the ceiling, a spanking bench, and a couple of other contraptions that weren't familiar to her. The couches were securely fastened to the floor, something that allowed people to have sex without worrying about sliding their couch into the people behind them.

She curled up next to Jesse on a couch right by the stage that Master Liam had saved for them and let her gaze wander over the crowd, only able to clearly see the people closest to the lights illuminating the elevated platform. There were a variety of couples, and most were engaged in some kind of play. She didn't know what to watch first: the man on his knees giving his Master a blowjob, the pretty brunette with her breasts bound in rope being fingered by her Master, or the Mistress in a long, elaborate ball gown with her submissive beneath the skirt, doing a damn good job of eating her pussy if her sighs of pleasure were any indication.

A sense of anticipation hung heavy in the air, and sex saturated her mind. Her own arousal was growing by the moment, helplessly pulled along in the sensual spell being woven by the couples around her. She'd never considered that watching someone have sex would turn her on so much. When Jesse brushed the side of her breast with his hand, she sighed.

"Do you like this, Dove?"

She nodded, unable to tear her gaze away from the Mistress quickly approaching her orgasm. Her beautiful skirt moved as the broad shoulders of her sub pressed her legs farther apart. Her body arched into a bow, her mouth opened in a soundless scream as the submissive did something to make the Mistress clutch frantically at his head beneath her skirt.

Jesse laughed softly. "You haven't even seen the main event yet. Masters Liam and Rory are the head submissive trainers for Wicked, and tonight Master Liam will be training one of his students. Master Liam loves an audience, which is probably why he and Master Rory share their submissives. That way there is always someone to appreciate their technique."

Her pulse sped up, and her pussy clenched as the Mistress wailed out her release. "They share?"

"Oh yes. For Master Liam and Master Rory, watching and being watched adds the spice they're addicted to."

"What spice are you addicted to?"

He leaned closer and softly brushed his lips over her forehead. "You. I crave you to the point where I'm almost savage. Being with you is very...intense."

Her heart ached for his words to be true. "Is intense good?"

Kissing his way gently down her face, he made her quiver deep down in her belly, her body a physical manifestation of her emotions. His kisses affected her to a soul-deep level. They were so controlled, yet they ghosted over her skin as he slowly made his way to her mouth. The soft down of his beard brushed against her in an entirely pleasurable stroke.

When he reached her lips, they both stilled, their breath mingling without their skin touching. "What do you think?" He ever so softly brushed her lips. "There is so much to show you, so many things for you to experience. I want to make every one of them the best they can be for you. Tonight is only the beginning. There is nothing you could do or want that would shock me."

She traced the seam of his lips with her tongue before replying. "What if I wanted to have sex in public?"

"Done."

"But—"

"No argument, Dove. If you want to be my submissive, you will respect my wishes, trust me to lead you." His tone gentled, turned to auditory sin. "Think about it. All the attention focused on you, enjoying your pleasure, being turned on by your cries as you're being turned on by Mistress Rebecca's release." He held her breast in his hand, rubbing his thumb over her hard nub. "No one here knows who you are. You can do anything you want, indulge in anything you want. I'll be here to protect you, to make sure no one harms you. Let yourself fly, Dove."

She turned to face him, her breathing irregular as more and more of the crowd began to play. His words tempted her, but she didn't want to fly alone. "Do you like playing in public, Master Jesse?"

He smiled and leaned forward to whisper in her ear. "The idea of showing you off, of letting the other Doms see what I have, how amazing you are, how beautifully you come, does turn me on." He took her hand and placed it on the warm leather covering his very hard erection. "See."

When she squeezed him, he groaned and nipped her ear. "Master, I'm yours to play with. Anything you want, I'll do." She meant it with every ounce of her being. While she couldn't give him the truth, she could give him herself.

A man cleared his throat, and they both looked up to find Master Liam standing next to the couch. He'd taken his shirt off, and she enjoyed his rough, masculine beauty. There was nothing soft about him, from the dark fur covering his chest down to his low-riding kilt, which emphasized the tendons angled to his groin. A lovely African American woman stood next to him with her head down and her hands folded in front of her. She wore a simple white cotton robe that hid her body in a demure manner that was at odds with the decadent revelry around them. Her hair was pulled off her face in long, thin dreadlocks, exposing her classic bone structure.

"Jesse, can I have a moment of your time?"

Her Master nodded and stood. Master Liam lifted his chin to his submissive. "Gloria, kneel next to the couch and wait for me. You may talk with Dove. Reassure her I'm not some savage, sex-starved beast."

Master Liam's submissive said in a mischievous voice, "But you told me to never lie, Sir."

"You'll pay for that, lass."

The two men moved a few feet away and began to talk in low voices. Master Liam's submissive peeked at Anya from beneath her lowered lashes. "Nice to meet you, Dove. You have the most beautiful hair, like spun gold." She had an accent that gave her words an exotic cadence.

"Thank you." Anya flushed and struggled for something to say.

Gloria gave her a gentle smile. "New to this, aren't you?"

She nodded. "I'm afraid I'm not sure what to do."

"You don't have to worry about that. Your Master will tell you what to do." Gloria sounded so peaceful, so sure. "Open yourself to the experience and trust him. Master Jesse is a good man, and he really likes you. As part of my training Master Liam and Master Rory have taught me a lot about reading body language. I can tell from the way Master Jesse looks at you, how he follows your every move, that he's fascinated by you."

Anya glanced at Jesse out of the corner of her eye; he was still talking with Master Liam. "I don't want to disappoint him."

"You are a beautiful woman. Skin like cream, full lips, and the kind of body men want beneath them." Gloria's full lips curved into a seductive smile. "The kind of body women want beneath them as well."

Anya stared at the submissive kneeling next to her, pretty sure the other woman had made a pass at her. Another first. "Umm, thank you. You're nice as well." She groaned and shook her head. "I'm sorry. This is all so new to me. I really do think you're pretty."

Gloria giggled, a surprisingly girlish sound. She leaned forward, placing her hand on Anya's knee. "Don't worry. We were all new once. Let me see if I can help you relax. Maybe if you know why I like this, you will understand. I love being watched, love knowing I'm turning other people on." Gloria's voice grew husky, and when she lightly caressed the skin just above Anya's knee, Anya didn't pull away, entranced by this confident, sexy woman. "I also love to watch, to see another woman filled with her Master's cock while my Master takes his pleasure with me. I like to look into her eyes and know we're feeling the same thing, the same pleasure, approaching the same indescribable bliss of our orgasm. That's what it's like for me when I'm with a woman for my Master's pleasure. I take great joy in knowing how to touch her, to play with her body in the same way I love my own being played with."

Gloria licked her lower lip, and Anya found herself wondering what the other woman's mouth tasted like. Though she'd admired other women before, she'd never been aroused by them. Being attracted to Gloria was strange and erotic. The thrill of the forbidden mingled with curiosity. While the other woman kept her touch light and teasing, Anya half wished she would stroke higher, to show Anya what she was missing. Out of the corner of her eye, she saw they were now the focus of a great deal of attention, including Master Jesse's and Master Liam's. The two men had stopped talking and were staring at them with raw lust.

"That's right. Do you see how much it turns our Masters

on to see us together? I imagine we're quite the visual treat, vanilla and chocolate if you will. When I'm up there, with Master Liam working on me, I'll be watching you with Master Jesse." She leaned closer still, the weight of her breasts brushing Anya's legs. "If that's all right with you."

It took her a moment to find her voice, but when she did, it still came out strangled. "Yes."

"You will feel how powerful it is to be connected to a crowd, to have their energy washing over you. I know it sounds silly, but I swear I can feel it when someone is watching me. It is amazing."

Anya lowered her head and peeked at Master Jesse, who watched her with a dark stare that tightened her body in a hard rush like he'd slammed his cock into her. Quickly looking away, she met the warm, seductive arousal in Gloria's dark eyes. Their skin rubbed together as Gloria entwined her hands with Anya's.

"Let me tell you a little secret. There is nothing I love more than eating another woman out after she's been filled with her Master's seed. To taste the mixture of arousal is wonderful, and I love how wet and soft a woman's cunt is, how swollen and hot, after a good fucking. Think about what it would be like to have Jesse holding you while my mouth works your body. I bet you have a very pretty, very sweet pussy."

Good Lord, Gloria could tempt the devil into sin. The erotic images she spun through Anya's head had her almost desperate to be touched. Before she could respond, their Masters returned, and Gloria sat back on her heels, her eyes lowered and once again the picture of demure obedience. Anya continued to stare at the other woman, unable to believe the wicked things the exotic beauty had whispered to her.

A deep, primal beat came through speakers hidden somewhere in the room, a cavernous industrial tone with lots of drums and bass. It somehow added to the atmosphere, made it seem even more dreamlike. Though even in her wickedest of dreams, Anya had never imagined being somewhere like this, with someone like Master Jesse.

Master Liam chuckled and gripped the back of Gloria's neck in a proprietary manner. "What has my naughty submissive been whispering to you, Dove?"

She swallowed hard and tore her gaze away from Gloria. Jesse sat down on the couch next to her, and his nostrils flared. "Whatever it was, it's gotten her so wet and aroused that I can smell it."

Embarrassed, turned on, and confused, she gratefully climbed onto her Master's lap when he held his arms open. As soon as she touched him, the discomfiture and confusion receded, helped in part by the hard cock beneath her ass. She was indeed wet, so wet that when her thighs pressed together against her pussy, her fluids dripped down the curve of her ass. Goodness, if Jesse touched her right now, she'd explode.

Master Liam turned, his erection obvious against his leather kilt. "Enjoy the show, Dove."

He gave her a naughty wink and grinned, making her feel a little more at ease. It was hard to be anxious around men who exuded such confidence.

Master Liam and Gloria made their way to the stage, and Jesse cupped her chin in his hand, making her look up at him. "Whatever did Gloria say to put you in such a state?"

"She...she..." Unable to get the words out, she silently pleaded with Jesse to not make her say them. However stupid it sounded, talking about it out loud would make her embarrassed. She looked into his eyes, begging him not to make her say it.

Unfortunately, the man looking back at her didn't have a trace of mercy for her plight. "Tell me what she said, or I will put you in a chastity belt and make you watch Gloria come over and over while you get nothing."

"She said she wanted to eat your cum out of my pussy."

His gaze became speculative. "And that turns you on?"

She buried her face against his chest, then gasped when he forced his hand between her legs. "Fuck, you are dripping wet." He pressed his palm against her sex, sealing it beneath his touch, and she cried out. "Oh yeah, you like that thought. While I would never let another man touch you, I must admit having Gloria between your legs is a rather pretty picture."

"Master, I don't know if I could do that." She stole a glance at him. "I don't want you— Gosh, this sounds stupid, but I don't want you to think I want someone other than you."

"Little one, I'm very secure in the knowledge you want me." He smiled and raised the hand that had been between her legs to her lips, painting them with her arousal. "But I also want to push you, to make you experience pleasures you'd never do on your own. That's part of what makes me a Dominant. I know you want it, but you're afraid to take that step on your own. If I feel it is what you need, it won't be your decision to make. You will bend to my will, and you will do whatever I tell you. If it's having that dusky beauty cleaning you of my seed, then you will spread your legs for her. If you don't, I will spread them for you with my cock still inside of you, and she will clean your juices off my balls with her clever tongue, neglecting you for my pleasure. And I will fucking love every minute of it because I'm sharing this with you. My submissive, my Dove."

Everything inside of her tightened. She pressed her thighs together and groaned at the pressure. She needed more, needed him inside her, needed to come over and over again. He must have seen her desperation, because he gave her a cold yet fiercely aroused smile that was more like a snarl.

"Don't even think about it."

"But—"

He spun her around so she straddled his lap backward, her back to his front, her legs looped over the outside of his thighs, exposing the edges of her slick pussy and soaked panties to the stage. She groaned and wiggled against him, silently pleading with him to let her have her release. He spread his legs, forcing hers to follow until she was as exposed as she could be to the stage.

On the platform Master Liam had already stripped

Gloria down and had her hands fastened to the chains dangling from the ceiling. Instead of the chains being silver, they were brass and had been cut and polished to gleam like the skin of a snake. The other woman had a beautiful, lean body with dark nipples and closely trimmed curls guarding her mound. When Master Liam stroked his hand over Gloria's hip, Anya loved how erotic the contrast of skin tones was. She wondered what it would look like when he fucked the other submissive, and groaned low in her throat.

Anya was vaguely aware of the other people in the room, but all her attention was split between Jesse at her back and the sight before her.

Master Liam was walking in a circle around Gloria, flicking her with a black leather flogger on her breasts, ass, and pussy. Each gentle blow brought a groan from the chained woman, and when Anya looked up at her face, she found Gloria watching her.

Jesse's lips ghosted over the sensitive skin of her ear. "Watch how her body responds to him, how she seeks his touch, bends into the blows instead of away." On the stage Master Liam kicked the woman's legs apart until she stood in a wide stance, her wet pussy exposed to the crowd. "He's not going to let her come for a long, long time."

Needy, wanton, Anya ground her bottom on his erection. The flogging continued, each slap coming harder, leaving a rising red blush all over the other woman's body. When Master Liam flicked the leather strands against Gloria's pussy, she cried out, her hips thrusting forward but her gaze never leaving Dove.

"See how she watches you? You're as much responsible for the honey dripping from her as Liam is. Watch how her gaze goes from your face to your breasts and down to your cunt." He reached around her and wrapped his hands into the strings of her panties. "Let's give her some of the prettiest pink pussy on earth to look at."

With a harsh jerk, he ripped the scrap of silk from between her legs, exposing her bare mound to the room. Gloria groaned and shuddered, a hungry look entering her gaze. Master Liam tossed the flogger off to the side and pulled a pair of nipple clamps out of a small pocket on his kilt. He played with the other woman's nipples in a way that had Anya moaning with need. When Jesse began to do the same to Anya, she thought she'd lose her mind. She sank into the sensation, struggling to keep her eyes open as Jesse whispered into her ear about how pretty her body was, how snug and tight her cunt would feel on his cock.

On the stage Master Liam had released Gloria from the chains and had her bent over the table, facing Dove. The other woman's gaze never wavered as the big Scotsman ran his hands over her reddened skin before giving her ass a brisk slap. The noise cracked through the air, and Anya started, then bit her lower lip hard enough to sting when Jesse moved one of his hands to her mound. He kept his fingers just above her slit and gently pressed his middle finger down, somehow feeling like he was touching her clit even though he was a good half inch away from that throbbing nub.

After a dozen spanks that had Gloria crying out and involuntarily trying to wiggle away, Master Liam picked up a bottle of oil and poured it down the curve of her bottom. Behind Anya, Jesse groaned deep in his throat. He pressed against her, his cock seated firmly against her cheeks.

"He's going to fuck her ass." Jesse sank his teeth into the side of her throat, and she stiffened, the pain mingling with the pleasure of his hand still plucking at her tender nipples and his finger caressing her smooth mound. "Someday I'm going to do the same to you, and you'll cry from the pain and pleasure of it."

Hell, she wanted him to do it right now. He could take her however he wanted as long as he filled the throbbing ache deep inside in the way only he could.

"Please, Master, please take me. I won't come, I promise. I need you inside of me."

He slid his finger down her slit and inside her, cursing when her body clamped on him. "If you come before I tell you, I will be very disappointed."

She was unable to form any coherent words as Jesse stroked his finger in and out of her pussy at the same pace that Master Liam was sliding his fingers in and out of Gloria's ass. Anya's orgasm built and built until she was shaking with the effort of not coming. "Jesse, Master, I can't hold back much longer."

He eased his fingers out and moved her over to the side long enough to open his leathers and pull out his big, very hard dick. Before she could draw a breath, he had her back on his lap, holding her up with his upper body strength.

"Guide me in."

She positioned the fat head of his dick at her entrance and cried out when he began to slowly lower her onto his thick erection. Inch by inch he filled her. When her dazed gaze returned to the stage, she watched Gloria's face contort with pain and pleasure as Master Liam began to shove his very big dick into her ass. Their eyes met, and a bolt of electricity seemed to surge between them, connecting them together, feeding Anya's arousal until she helplessly milked Jesse's cock with her delicate muscles.

Behind her Jesse cursed and set a brutal pace, raising her up and down on his cock as if she were a doll, using the tight sheath of her pussy for his own pleasure.

"Dove, I'm going to come inside of you, fill you up fast and hard. Then, after Gloria has licked you clean, made you come all over her face, I'm going to fuck you again."

"God, yes."

Anya panted, and Master Liam watched them, his jaw clenched as he eased in and out of Gloria at a much slower, gentler pace. The other woman writhed beneath him, her eyes barely open as he worked her. It was so damn hot watching them have sex. Like Gloria had said, the knowledge that the other woman was feeling what she felt left Anya in an almost mindless state. There wasn't room for anything more than pleasure.

Still, Anya wanted to come very badly, and that wouldn't happen until after she served her Master. She reached down to where Jesse's cock shuttled in and out of her pussy, and began to gently rub and tug at his balls.

"Fuck, that's it, baby. Make me come."

She could feel his testicles draw up tight beneath her fingers, his body losing its rhythm as he pounded into her. Desperate to please him, to do as he commanded, she stroked a finger down his perineum and pressed against the entrance between his cheeks. He made a strangled cry and lunged into her, holding her hips so tight she was sure she'd have bruises there tomorrow.

Not that she gave one flying fuck. He could cover her in bruises, and she'd happily take them all, wear them with pride as symbols of his pleasure in her. Each mark would be a testament to how good she made him feel.

She held perfectly still, her attention on Gloria as Jesse filled her up with his cum. The jerking of his dick inside her was delicious torture, and her inability to join him made her feel savage. She raked her nails down his thighs, and he groaned before capturing her wrists in his hands.

"Behave."

On the stage Master Liam pulled out of Gloria, his condom-covered dick shiny with the oil used to ease his passage. He grabbed a handful of Gloria's hair and awkwardly dragged her across the stage. He stepped off first and brought Gloria down, pushing her onto her hands and knees. Jesse pulled out of Anya but didn't move her much, just sliding his still-hard dick between her butt cheeks. He gripped her thighs and widened his legs, forcing her to spread almost to the point of making her hips ache.

Not that she cared. The ravenous gleam in Gloria's eyes had her heart beating triple time.

Master Liam bent over and gave Gloria's ass a hard slap. "Go clean Dove for her Master."

The beautiful black woman crawled across the floor like

a panther, licking her full lips in a manner that had Anya twitching and moaning. Once Gloria was between her legs, Master Liam knelt behind her and lifted his kilt, spreading her ass open with one hand.

Looking up at Anya, Gloria began to lick the soft crease where her thigh met her sex, and Anya's empty sheath contracted, pushing out some of the cum Jesse had put inside her. Gloria sighed and then sealed her mouth over Anya's pussy, sucking hard. Her lips felt so soft and her tongue smaller than what Anya was used to, a delicate swipe that made her toes curl.

Master Liam slammed himself into Gloria without preamble, making the woman grunt against Anya's swollen flesh. Jesse groaned and grabbed Anya's wrists, pinning them to his hips while Gloria nibbled and sucked at her flesh, sticking her tongue inside Anya's sheath and eating every trace of seed she could find. Then she worked her way up to Anya's clit, each thrust from Liam pressing her face hard into Anya's wet flesh.

Jesse rocked between the curves of her ass cheeks, making her yearn to have him there like Gloria had her Master. She looked down, mesmerized by the sight of the woman's dark lips sealing over her swollen clit, the sensation of her teeth nibbling at the very tip. Master Liam swore and groaned, his strain from holding back his own orgasm showing in the ruthless way he fucked Gloria.

It all began to blur together: Gloria's mouth, the slap of Master Liam's hips hitting Gloria's ass, and finally Jesse's lips against Anya's ear. Everything felt so good, Anya never wanted it to stop, but she would die of pleasure if it didn't. "Come for me, Dove. Make that greedy bitch lick up every drop."

Gloria sucked hard on her clit, working with her teeth and tongue until Anya arched against her. One final swipe of the other woman's tongue, and Anya lost herself in bliss, falling over the edge into her release, her body shaking against her Master as he held her tight, held her safe in the middle of the storm of sensations. He talked her through what had to be the longest orgasm of her life, telling her how beautiful she was, how proud he was of her for trusting him, and how much he wanted her.

Master Liam said through gritted teeth, "Clean his balls, girl, and come while you do it."

Gloria complied, and her harsh cries became muffled as her head worked below Anya's tender pussy, her dreads tickling Anya's skin. Jesse tensed; his hips surged forward. He grabbed Anya's breasts and began to kneed them, rough movements that roused her own passion. She watched, fascinated as Master Liam looked between her breasts, pussy, and Gloria's busy head, his face tensing, his whole body going tight.

With a roar, Master Liam jerked and strained against Gloria, pulling her up toward him so that he held her tight to his chest while he emptied himself into her willing body.

Jesse lifted Anya off his lap and turned her around. Without being asked, she straddled him and tilted her hips, sliding him into her channel. They both froze, their bodies slick against each other with sweat. God, when he looked at her like he was now, she felt so connected to him, like their souls were brushing together as well as their bodies.

He pushed her back so he could grab her breasts, squeezing them hard enough to hurt. The pain made her jerk her hips, and his long dick sank even deeper, far enough to make her body ache from the strain of taking him.

She loved it.

"You've been a good girl, Dove. Ride me until you come."

She placed her hands on his shoulders, going slow, taking her time with him. A delicious numbness fuzzed her nerves, almost like she was floating. Then she met his gaze. The desire and the possession there had her groaning. He was marking her as his, publicly, in a primal way that told the other Doms to back off. She might as well be wearing his collar, because she didn't want anyone except him. The thought of being his submissive, his woman made her heart pound even harder.

He shifted so her clit bumped over his pelvis, the rough hair there scratching against her swollen nub in a delicious way. She somehow felt even more sensitive after Gloria's mouth had been on her. Every stroke with Jesse was a dream of pleasure, an experience she would crave for the rest of her life.

When he pulled her down to kiss her, his hand went to the back of her neck like Master Liam had held Gloria. A collar made out of flesh. She moaned against him, eagerly opening her mouth, then sucked on his tongue. Never before had she felt so alive. The wonderful building sensation of her orgasm slowly rolled through her, matching the long, unhurried pace of their strokes.

When Jesse grabbed her ass, she gasped and began to move faster. He spread her cheeks with his hands, and suddenly a wet tongue licked at her anus. She jumped, but Jesse held her tight, not letting her move away, making her kiss him with savage nips at her mouth. He held Anya open wider, and the tongue was replaced with two slender fingers.

Bucking against Jesse, she held him tight, burying her face against his neck and crying out. He began to thrust beneath her, slamming into her body and hitting her cervix with a muscle-tightening rhythm. The fingers in her bottom sped up and began to scissor open, widening her back passage. Is this what Jesse would do before he took her ass? Get her so worked up like this, to the point where she was begging him to take her back there?

"Dove, come for me."

She ground her pelvis into his in a tight circle, mashing her clit against him, then tensing. When the fingers in her ass withdrew, leaving a stinging burn behind, she lost control. Her shout had to have raised the roof because it came from the bottom of her soul. Jesse swore viciously and held her still, making her feel the pulsing of his dick inside her as he came again. She groaned at each twitch, sensitized to the point of it being too much.

As if he understood, Jesse didn't pull out after he finished, instead holding her to his chest. He wrapped his arms around her, and someone placed a blanket over her shoulders. It was warm and smelled faintly of vanilla. A relaxing and comforting sensation that, when combined with Jesse holding her so close, made her instantly sleepy.

He shifted her and slowly pulled out. She rose so he could tuck himself back into his leathers, then settled against him with a sigh, so glad she could finally just relax. Never in a million years did she think she'd do something as hedonistic, as wonderful as the night Jesse had just given her. With his presence, his constant reassurance, his control of her, he allowed Anya to immerse herself in the moment. Anything she did was with his blessing and for his pleasure, making what had already been an incredible sexual experience border on nirvana. The world drifted by, and she lost herself in the gentle sound of Jesse's voice as he talked with people around them, his occasional soft laughter rumbling against her ear like distant thunder. Through all of it, he never stopped touching her, making her feel pampered and loved.

CHAPTER NINE

Jesse pulled past the gates leading to his home and took a deep breath of the spring air, the top down on his Jaguar and some classic rock playing on the speakers. He felt remarkably good, almost revived, and he who knew to thank for that.

The beautiful, amazing young woman who wouldn't stop lying to him.

He'd learned a long time ago that one lie led to another and sooner or later that house of cards came falling down. It was a painful lesson he was going to impart to Anya next Friday if he didn't get her to admit she was also Dove this week. To aid him in his quest, he'd switched around his schedule so he could come home two hours early every day.

His personal assistant had practically cheered him when he said he was taking some time off, and he'd realized he hadn't had a real a vacation in five years. Oh, he'd taken the boys to visit family across the US, but they hadn't gone anywhere fun just for the hell of it. First because the boys had been too young, then because he couldn't face returning to some of his favorite vacation spots without his wife.

Carol loved to travel and had dragged him all over the globe before she passed, showing him things he never would have found on his own. She'd been a free spirit, someone whose life had burned bright and fierce, then ended all too soon. If she was watching over him—and he knew she was—she'd be rolling her eyes and telling him it was about time he got his head out of his ass.

And Carol would have loved Anya. Despite their physical differences and personalities, there was a streak of sweetness in both their souls. Anya had a gentler spirit than Carol, and that worked out well with Mark and Teddy. God knows they tried his patience in the way only little boys could. They weren't bad; they were...active.

Very active.

Carol would have also loved Anya's plan to go to Paris for the summer, and would have encouraged her every step of the way.

He turned the car toward the main house, driving out from beneath the black walnut trees that showed bright green buds all over in the sunlight. The stately manor Carol had fallen in love with at first sight stood on the top of a gentle rise, the undulating ribbon of the river flowing in the distance. He'd found himself thinking of his wife a lot lately. Instead of it being the usual sorrowful memories or thoughts of what they wouldn't have together, it was of the good times they'd had.

Paving stones crunched beneath his tires as he pulled up to the front of the house and put the Jag into park. Hopefully Anya was home with the boys. He knew from the pictures she sent him at work every day that she liked to take them out, to expose them to other children and new things. Much better than their last nanny, who'd been a bit of a hermit and hardly ever took the boys anywhere.

After taking off his suit coat, he slung it over his shoulder and tried to tell his body that just because he was going to see Anya didn't mean anything was going to happen. He prayed she would take the olive branch he was offering and open up to him. Last Saturday he'd wanted nothing more in the world than to take her home with him, to have her in his bed and in his arms, but she'd driven home alone and so had he.

All because of a stupid lie.

He went inside and tossed his briefcase next to the antique coatrack in the foyer and looked down the two hallways branching off. From somewhere to the right he could hear their voices, and he followed them, a smile tilting his lips. Anya hadn't realized it, but last night, she'd used her normal voice with him at the atrium and thereafter. Anger ghosted over him at how shaken up she'd been after her encounter with Bryan, and he resolved to have a word with the other man.

Turning the corner, he came to the entrance of the kitchen and stopped, his heart doing a painful thump in his chest.

Teddy, the younger twin with flaxen blond curls, was standing on a stool next to the big slate island in the middle of the kitchen. To his right, his brother, Mark, with his amber-blond hair, was cutting a cookie from a rolled-out piece of dough. Anya was leaning over him, helping him press down into the dough. A foil-covered baking tray lay nearby, and half a dozen misshapen cookies lay on it.

Anya wasn't wearing her ridiculous glasses. She still wore the frumpy sweatpants, but the matching sweatshirt lay over the back of a chair at the kitchen table. Dressed in a pink T-shirt that showed the magnificent swell of her breasts, she presented a picture of sexy domestic tranquility that should have been odd but wasn't. How a woman could at once be nurturing and sensual was part of the feminine mystique that had baffled and entranced men since the beginning of time.

Hating to break the comfortable domestic atmosphere, he cleared his throat. "What are we making?"

"Daddy!"

His boys both raced over to him and gave him hugs that covered him in bits of dough and flour. He scooped them up, grunting and amazed anew at how quickly they grew, and watched Anya dash across the room and throw her sweatshirt on, inside out and backward.

"Hello, Mr. Shaw. I didn't expect you home so soon." Her voice had a slight tremble to it, and she avoided his gaze.

Bemused, he walked toward her with a boy on either hip. She started to back up, her beautiful blue-gray eyes finally meeting his and going wide, but he stopped before he reached her. He had to remind himself that in Anya's mind, he was still the clueless boss who didn't know her real identity. Now he had to walk a thin line between getting her to open up to him and not coming on too heavy. Fuck, he hated when things got complicated like this, but real life was never easy.

Hefting the boys on his hips, he asked them, "Who can tell me what Anya did wrong?"

She blanched and turned to reach for her glasses on the kitchen table. Before she could put them on, Teddy reached out and grabbed the tag on her shirt, pulling it. "Anya put her inside on her outside!"

Mark giggled and slid out of his arms. "Anya, you're silly. Your backside is on your front side."

Giving the boys a relieved smile, she pulled out the neck of her shirt and looked down. "I guess I did." She straightened and held her glasses so tight her knuckles turned white. "I'll just leave you guys—"

"Actually, I was hoping you could stay and help me out."

She chewed her bottom lip, moving quickly past him to pluck Mark off the counter before he could grab an unbaked cookie off the sheet. "With what, Mr. Shaw?"

"Call me Jesse."

She froze, then cleared her throat. "I don't know if that's appropriate."

He laughed while Teddy slid out of his arms to join Mark at the counter, the boys standing on stools and cutting out different cookie shapes. "Anya, it's fine. I promise I won't fire you for using my name. Besides, I need you to help me out today."

She kept her back to him, a slight tremble running through her shoulders as she rolled out the dough. Damn, he hadn't meant to throw her this off-balance. He needed to calm her down, but the only way to do that was by making her get used to his presence.

He lowered his voice to a dramatic whisper. "I need to take the boys to pick out a birthday present for their cousin, Neil."

She paused in her rolling. "To a t-o-y-s-t-o-r-e?" He nodded, then realized she couldn't see him and came over to the island, putting himself on the other side. "Yeah. I'm sure you understand why I don't dare attempt this alone. Usually my mom comes along, but she's out on a hot date." He made a gagging sound.

Anya giggled but still wouldn't look up at him. "Your mother is in her fifties, not dead."

"True, but I'd rather believe she has lived a chaste life all these years."

"Then how did you come along?"

"Immaculate conception."

Now she did laugh, and it was her real, true laugh. The one he pulled so easily from her at Wicked. Inappropriate thoughts to have around his children flashed through his mind, and he quickly moved closer to the island so she wouldn't see the growing bulge in his pants. "I'm going to go upstairs and wash up and change. Do you think you and the boys will be ready by the time I get done?"

"Sure, these cookies need to chill before we bake them anyways." She gave him a shy glance. "We'll be waiting for you."

—✻—

The next day Jesse spent the afternoon with Anya and the boys at the local park, and he was amazed anew at her energy and vibrancy. The day after that, they took the boys to the Smithsonian, and the next spent at home at the stables. A new foal had been born, and the boys thought the little horse's antics were the funniest things ever. His heart had melted a million times over watching Anya explain the world to his boys, helping them navigate its dangers without being overbearing or harsh. He knew part of her aptitude with children came from having helped her own single father raise her brothers, but most of it was just her.

She seemed to make the world brighter by being in it, and keeping his cool was getting harder and harder. He knew she'd caught him looking at her a couple of times with something more than friendship in his gaze. He sure as shit had caught her staring at him with longing. He'd had to wear his T-shirt untucked whenever he was around her, because everything about her turned him on.

Now they were both tucking the boys into bed after spending the day with them at an indoor arcade. Full of pizza and exhausted, for once, Mark and Teddy went to bed without a complaint. The way they both hugged Anya without reservation made him wish he could do the same. She wore her hair in a long braid tonight, and it hung down over her shoulder, tickling Mark's arm.

The boys blew him a kiss, and he told them good night, shutting the door after Anya with a sigh.

"I need a drink."

Anya giggled and slumped against the wall across from him. "Thank God they wanted you to do that dance game with them and not me."

He grimaced at the memory of her laughing until she cried as he tried to emulate the dance moves his five-year-olds did with such ease. Okay, so dancing might not be his thing, but he knew other ways of moving that would blow her mind. Lust flared through him, catching as easily as gas-soaked rags tossed into a bonfire. She was so close, all warm and soft. Fuck, he could even smell her.

Her laughter died away, and she wet her lower lip with a sweep of her tongue. He'd give anything to know what she was thinking right now. Was she looking at him as a sleazy guy who hit on his nanny while he had sex with another woman on the weekends, or was she seeing him as her Master?

She cleared her throat. "So, uh, want me to get you a drink? You're a vodka-tonic man, right?"

To his knowledge he'd never had her make a drink for him, except for the vodka tonic she'd brought him at Wicked. The thought of kissing the raspberry from between her plump lips had him gripping his hands into fists to keep from grabbing her and tongue fucking her mouth until she told him the truth.

But he couldn't. She had to be honest with him. She had to make that first move.

Please, God, let her make that first move.

Giving her a confused look, he nodded. "Yeah. How did you know that?"

Scarlet flooded her cheeks, and she shrugged. "Your bar is stocked with it downstairs, and you usually have a small glass after work."

Disappointment twisted through his stomach, and he wished just once she would trust him enough to admit her lies. "Well, I can't exactly order you to go get one, can I? I mean, you're my nanny, not my slave."

She stared at him, the whites of her eyes showing. "No, that wouldn't be proper."

Brushing past her, wanting to shake her and tell her he knew she was Dove, he smiled at her. "Probably not. You going to join me?"

Shaking her head, she backed away so fast she almost ran into the small table against the wall in the hallway. "I want to, but...it's just...no, that's not a good idea."

Clenching his jaw, he nodded. "Okay. Good night, Anya. Thanks for all the help these past few days. I can't remember when I've seen my boys so happy."

She mumbled something and fled, leaving him with an aching dick, an empty heart, and disappointment.

This shit had to stop.

CHAPTER TEN

Anya smiled at Sunny and adjusted the dress she'd altered for her friend. "There. That looks much better."

Sunny gave a weary sigh and nodded. "Thank you so much. I've lost a bunch of weight recently, and my clothes are hanging off of me. Thing is, I don't want to lose it, but I have some kind of freakishly high metabolism. It seems to have gone into overdrive lately."

Looking closer, Anya noticed the circles beneath Sunny's eyes. "You look tired."

"I am tired. School has been kicking my ass, and I've had these awful stress headaches. Plus my mom... Well, let's say she hasn't been making things easier."

"I hear you on that one. Well, spring semester is almost over, right?"

"Yes, thank God." Sunny took a deep breath and grabbed her makeup brush off the dressing room table. "You look very pretty tonight."

Anya ran her hand over her flowing white dress, loving the way it glimmered with her every breath. Two sheer gatherings of the iridescent cloth attached to the bodice in the valley between her breasts, and the skirt was short enough to show her cheeks if she bent over. "I hope Master Jesse likes it."

"I think you could wear a sack and he'd like it. That man is gaga over you. I've never seen him show this much interest in anyone. Usually it's the submissives that are perusing him, not the other way around. Mark my words. He'll probably offer you his collar sooner than later."

She flushed and fingered her hips where the bruises from his big hands gripping her while he fucked her had almost faded away. "Yeah, well, we'll see."

She didn't want to reveal her secret to Sunny. Having the other woman know what a slimeball she was being wouldn't help anything other than increasing her own self-loathing. Shoving her conflicted feelings away, she stood and adjusted the strap of her top.

"Time to go. You ready?"

Sunny made a face in the mirror and dabbed at her crimson lipstick. "Ready as I'll ever be."

——✻——

It was the last fifteen minutes of her shift, and Jesse had yet to appear. Her good mood had slowly sunk like a deflating balloon. Oh, the crowd was as nice as ever, and she'd met a group of submissives who had been very friendly and answered a lot of her questions, but she missed him. Without Jesse watching over her, she felt vulnerable. Everything wasn't quite as fun as it had been when he was here. After spending so much time with him this week, she was in danger of falling head over heels with him. In fact, she already liked him way more than she should. Enough that she considered telling him the truth, and enough that she couldn't take it if she did and he hated her.

A Mistress thanked her for the drink, and Anya curtseyed, having learned the woman liked it and would tip better if she did. She filled her last drink order and wandered back to the bar. Sunny gave her a strained smile while rubbing her temples. "Shit, I thought this night would never end."

"No kidding." Anya turned so she could keep an eye on the floor, wondering where the hell Jesse was. "Your head still hurting?"

"Like muskrats are making a den in my skull."

A man's deep voice came from over her shoulder. "Woman, you need to go to a doctor."

Anya turned to find Master Hawk glowering at the pretty bartender. After seeing Hawk in a dozen action movies, she found it rather odd to be standing next to him. While Jesse was still the hottest man on earth, she had to admit the smooth, bronze expanse of Hawk's muscled chest was rather nice to look at through the opening of his black leather vest.

Sunny closed her eyes, the strain she was under showing in the tight line of her jaw. "I'm okay."

Hawk moved so he stood as close to Sunny as he could with the bar between them. "I know you don't like taking painkillers—"

"Back off!" Several heads turned their way, and Sunny let out a weary sigh. "Please, Hawk, not tonight."

Anya started to move away, wanting to give them their privacy, but Hawk turned his angry gaze on her. "Jesse is waiting for you in room sixteen on the second floor."

Elation filled her even as she kept a worried eye on Sunny. "Thank you. Sunny, I have to agree with Master Hawk. If your headaches are making you lose weight—"

Hawk let out a low growl. "You're losing weight?"

Sunny shot her a nasty look. "I'm fine. Hawk, why don't you go fuck Goddess and leave me alone."

Anya gasped, not used to seeing her friend this mean. "Sunny."

The other woman looked away, and Hawk turned to Anya. "Go to Master Jesse, Dove. I will make sure Sunny is taken care of."

She beat a hasty retreat, not wanting to be there when the storm clouds building between Sunny and Hawk broke. Things would be so much easier if Sunny told Hawk she was in love with him, but Anya sure as heck wasn't in any position to speak about honesty. A dozen times this week she'd almost mustered the courage to tell Jesse, only to wimp out at the last moment. Maybe after tonight she would tell him. Have one last good memory with him before he never wanted to see her again.

After getting lost twice and having to ask a passing Mistress for directions, she finally made it to room sixteen. Her heart hammered in her throat, and she knocked on the door. A few moments later Jesse opened it and stared down at her, his expression unreadable. No, not totally unreadable; for a second she thought she saw real anger tighten his features. The coldness in his gaze was so different from how he usually looked at her that for one moment she wondered if somehow he'd found out about her deception.

When he didn't speak, only continued to give her that intense look, she took a step back. "I'm sorry I was late. Please don't be mad at me."

He didn't say anything but stepped aside so she could enter. When she got a good look at the room, a shiver of apprehension skittered up her spine. It looked like she was in some type of police interrogation room, complete with a table, two chairs, and a video camera in the upper corner. There was even a two-way mirror, and she hoped no one was beyond it. Sitting on a stainless steel table along one wall were a variety of whips, canes, and other implements she didn't even have a name for.

Swallowing hard, she backed up until the edge of a chair hit her knees. She looked behind her and noticed the chair had restraints on the arms and legs, but that the middle of the seat was missing. When she realized why it wouldn't be there and what parts of her body the chair would expose to his touch, a flush of heat pushed away her unease.

"Master, do you want me to sit here?"

He nodded and waited until she'd positioned herself, then came over and efficiently strapped her in place. Efficient was the only word she could use to describe his touch. He didn't caress her or even look at her. In fact he seemed to be touching her as little as possible. She jerked at the restraints around her arms, but they didn't move an inch. The leather was hard, unforgiving against her skin, and bit into her wrists.

"Please talk to me. You're scaring me."

He ignored her and moved one of the regular chairs from the other side of the table and brought it over in front of her. He took a seat, his knees almost touching hers as he leaned back and folded his hands over his stomach. She searched his face for something to tell her it was okay, but she couldn't find anything to reassure her.

She forced a laugh and gave him a coquettish look. "Do I have to earn my way out?"

Instead of smiling at her, his expression grew even darker. When minutes passed by and he did nothing more than stare, her unease grew. He just stared at her with a flat, cold look. The laughing, smiling man that had brought her so much pleasure was gone, leaving behind a guy she didn't recognize. Unease spooled out in her belly, making her heart pound with a trace of real fear.

"Untie me. I don't want to do this." She jerked at the restraints, but the chair didn't even move. "Let me go! Jesse, what is wrong with you?"

He took a slow breath, the air pouring into his body seeming to flame the anger banked in his gaze to a conflagration that burned her.

"The question is, what is wrong with you, Anya? How long were you going to fuck me and then go back to my home, watch my children, and lie to me? Were you ever going to tell me the truth? Or were you going to keep on playing me, then vanish off to Paris?"

Oh God.

His unusual actions of the week before finally made sense. No wonder he seemed to seek her out after pretty much ignoring her for the entire time she'd worked for him She thought it was because he genuinely needed her help with the boys, or maybe he enjoyed her company.

She'd been such a fool.

"How long have you known?"

"Long enough. My mom wanted me to invite you to

dinner, and I went to the carriage house to ask you. All your costumes were on display, easily seen through the French doors. To say I was shocked, hurt, and really fucking pissed is an understatement."

All the breath left her body in a painful rush, and she struggled to get free, to cover her face, to hide her shame and fear from him. The more she struggled, the tighter the bonds got until her wrist and ankles hurt. Her brain yelled at her to say something, to explain herself and get him to let her go. Her heart raced, and the metallic taste of blood flavored her mouth as she bit her lip.

He leaned forward, resting his elbows on his knees in a deceptively relaxed pose. "I gave you every opportunity to come clean this week, to tell me the truth. But you continued to lie. You played me for a fool. I trusted you. In fact I thought Dove"—his lips curled in disgust, and she died inside—"was one of the most honest, intriguing submissives I've ever met, but it was all bullshit. You never intended this to be anything more than a fling."

"It wasn't like that!"

"Right. When I was inside of you, looking into your eyes, I thought I saw something beautiful." Hurt replaced the anger, and for a moment, he looked weary. "What did I ever do to you that would make you want to deceive me like this? Why didn't you tell me?"

Everything closed in on her, choking the air out of her, filling her with panic and shame. "Please, let me go. I'll go back to your place right away and get my things, or you can have them sent to my dad's house, just please let me go!"

She screamed the last word into his face, and his eyes cleared. He sat back and rubbed his face. His anger faded a bit, and he frowned at her. "Do you think I'm going to hurt you?"

She jerked at the bonds repeatedly, struggling to get free. "Let me go!"

"Is that the kind of man you think I am?"

"Let me go!"

She jerked against the bonds, and the chair rocked with her struggles. Her wrists burned and her arms ached, but she didn't care. She wanted to run away, to go hide from her shame, to never have to see him look at her with such hurt and betrayal again. The fact she was a liar, a manipulative bitch who hurt him to satisfy her own selfish needs, cut at her soul.

"Anya, calm down. You're hurting yourself."

"Ivy, damn you! Ivy!" She screamed her safe word at him so hard her throat hurt, but her words had their intended effect.

He reached over and unstrapped her wrist. As soon as her hand was free, she shoved him away and fumbled with the other strap, her wrist stinging and burning. Unfortunately her hand was shaking so bad she couldn't manipulate the simple pull and release. Her hair hung in her face, obscuring her view as she jerked at the restraint.

He hated her, and she deserved it.

"Dove, Anya, whatever the hell your name is. Stay still so I can unstrap you." He deftly freed her, and she scrambled away from him, slamming her hip into the table with a painful *thud*, then bouncing off of it. He followed her, but she fled, trying to put the table between them. He simply slid across the surface to her side and reached for her. He managed to grab her arm before she raked at his hand with her nails.

He froze and closed his eyes.

"Don't touch me!" She was backed into a corner now. She grabbed one of the canes off the nearby table, brandishing it in front of her.

"Anya, I'm sorry. I didn't mean for it to go like this. I just wanted to get you to talk to me."

"You tied me up in that horrible chair!"

He roughly ran his hands through his hair. "What was I supposed to do? I tried to get you to tell me all week! Being nice wasn't working, so I had to try something else."

"Goddamn you, I didn't want to lie to you!"

"Then why did you?" He batted the cane away, the metal tip clattering against the cement floor.

A sob stuck in her throat, and she shoved at his arms, kicking at him and trying to get away. "Leave me alone!"

"Shh." He picked her up and almost dropped her as she struggled. "Anya, let me hold you so you can calm down and listen to me."

"No! You're going to put me back in that chair. You had no right!"

"I'm sorry. I handled this badly." He sat down on the floor and dragged her with him, trapping her struggling body with his strong legs. "Stop fighting me. I'm not going to hurt you. I would never hurt you."

She shuddered and went limp. It didn't matter what she said, what she did, he wasn't going to let her go until he was done with her. All she could do was endure until he finished ripping her a new one. Her heart ached, and even now she yearned for his touch. God, this was so messed up.

She was so messed up.

"If you don't want to hurt me, let me go."

"I wish I could," he muttered while lifting her right wrist, his face going pale at the deep red and purple mark from the strap against her flesh.

"Why did you do this to me? Why didn't you tell me you knew?" She hated how her voice sounded like a hurt little girl's. She wished she sounded stronger, was strong enough to not crave the reassurance of his touch even now.

He gave her a sharp look and brought her wrist to his mouth, placing gentle kisses over her abraded skin. The scent of his cologne and laundry detergent enveloped her. "I could ask you the same thing."

"I... What was I supposed to say? Hi, Jesse. I know I'm your nanny, but I would also love to be your submissive? When I look at you, I want to kiss you until neither of us can breathe? I want you more than I've ever wanted anyone?" Now it was his turn to stay silent, but he continued to press oh-so-soft kisses against her wrist. "It doesn't matter now. I'll stay until you can find a new nanny, but you won't have to see me. I'll make sure to leave as soon as you're home."

She took a deep breath, tears slipping from her eyes and rolling down her mask. With her free hand she peeled it off and threw it onto the table, then pulled her hair forward so he couldn't see her face. Nothing made any sense right now, and all the justifications she'd come up with sounded as weak as she felt.

"Anya." He loosened his hold until he was cradling her in his arms instead of restraining her. "I didn't mean to hurt you. I'm sorry."

"Me too." She took a shuddering breath and tried to muster the strength to leave his arms, but she couldn't. "I'm so sorry, Jesse. If I could take it all back, I would."

He brushed her hair from her face, capturing her chin in his hand when she tried to look away. To her surprise he leaned down and kissed away the tears trailing down her jaw, the soft brush of his beard against her face making her close her eyes. His lips trailed closer to her own, and he stilled, his breath washing over her mouth.

"You're so young. I shouldn't be doing this, but I can't resist you, Anya."

His lips drifted over hers and brought more comfort than passion. She attempted to pull back, but he wouldn't let her. That started a low burn in her belly. She tried to fight it, tried to resist the need to seek his forgiveness, but when he gently cupped her cheek and began to seduce her mouth with his own, she was lost.

He was so careful, so gentle with his kiss, nibbling against her mouth and coaxing her lips open so he could suck on her tongue in a way that made her toes curl. She could taste the salt of her tears on his lips, and his grip on her firmed when she tentatively stroked her tongue against his.

With a groan he pulled away. "No, we can't do this."

Anger had her struggling to get away from him again. "Then stop kissing me like I mean something. It's not fair, Jesse."

"That's not what I meant." He stared down at her, brushing her hair back and examining her features. "How could I miss how beautiful you are?"

Thrown off-balance, she frowned up at him. "You never really looked at me."

"I'm a fool."

"Yeah, well, so am I. Please let me go." She held his gaze, willing him to see the sincerity of her words. "Thank you for forgiving me, but I can't— I just...I can't be around you."

"I understand." He loosened his hold and helped her to stand up before rising next to her. "I don't want you to stop being my nanny. The boys love you, and you're so good with them. And I don't expect you to stop working here either. I'm guessing you're going to use the money from this job for Paris?"

She stepped away from him and nodded. "Yes. I'll be leaving in two weeks."

He took a deep breath. "I have a proposal for you."

"What?"

"You stay on as my nanny and continue working at Wicked. I won't treat you as anything other than a valued employee." Her heart sank, but before she could say anything, he continued. "Or you can do all of the above, and if you're willing, I'd like to have you as my submissive for the next two weeks. After the boys go to bed at night, you'll stay with me. I'll have the guest room adjacent to mine set up so the boys will think you're spending the night like their grandma does. Please, Anya. I want you chained to my bed. I want you to wake up to my face buried between your legs. I want to wake up to you riding my cock. But most of all I want you in my arms when the day finally ends and we both fall asleep. We don't have much time, and I'm selfish when it comes to you."

"I don't understand." She moved away from him, searching for her discarded mask. Oh God, his offer was tempting, but she was so messed up right now she wasn't sure what to think. "Why would you want that? Why would you want me? I lied to you. I'm a terrible person."

"Anya, you aren't a terrible person. You are one of the most amazing, kind, and loving women I've ever had the pleasure of meeting." He sighed and ran his hands through his hair. "Look, I know how short life is, how every minute is precious. I don't want to waste the time I do have with you."

She found her mask and held it between her fingers, wiping at the stains left by her tears. "I don't know, Jesse."

He came up behind her and wrapped his arms around her, his chin resting on top of her head. "Just think about it. Why don't we head home? You don't have to give me your answer right away, but I want to let you know the offer is out there. I hope you'll take it."

"Why me? I mean, you're so amazing, you could have anyone you want."

"Anya, you don't see very clearly either, do you? *You* are what I want." He turned her around and wiped away a tear. "Come on. I'll follow you home."

CHAPTER ELEVEN

Anya pulled into the garage attached to the carriage house, her gaze flicking to her rearview mirror, waiting for Jesse's car to appear. She turned off the engine and wished she knew what to do. The headlights from his car flashed over the garage. To her surprise instead of driving past and on to the main house, Jesse parked his car and got out, looking unbelievably handsome in the moonlight.

When he didn't move from the side of his car, she finally got out of her own, hauling her bag after her. After shutting her door, she looked up and found him watching her with an intensity that sent a wave of desire through her. All week she'd been anticipating this night, dreaming about it, but never would have thought it would end like this.

Biting her lower lip, she glanced at the door leading into the carriage house, then back to Jesse. Now that her secret was out, she didn't see any reason not to ask him for what she wanted, what she needed. Still, if he said no, it would hurt. Maybe she shouldn't ask him. Maybe he wouldn't want to do anything with her in his home. True the boys were with their grandmother right now, and Jesse had said he wanted her to move into the main house, but what if he'd only said that in the heat of the moment?

Oh God, what if he was thinking about firing her?

Screwing up her courage, she looked between him and the concrete floor of the garage when she said, "Would you like to come in for a drink?"

He took a step forward, then crossed his arms. "I shouldn't."

"Oh, okay." Unable to face his rejection, she turned and started toward the house, but the grit of footsteps had her pausing and turning to look over her shoulder. Jesse strode into the garage, an intense and almost desperate look on his face.

"Tell me to leave, Anya. If you don't want to do this, I'll understand." He stopped a pace away, his hands clenched and his body radiating tension.

Remembering his words about life being too short, and knowing her time with him was limited, she found the courage to whisper, "Stay."

He nodded and took her bag from her. She hoped he didn't notice how badly her hands were trembling when she unlocked the door and let them in, then flicked the light switch so the small living area became bathed in a warm golden glow. He followed her in, and she marveled at having him here, in her house, but not as her boss.

As her Master.

He tossed her bag onto a chair and strode over to her before grabbing her wrists and examining them in the light. "I should be whipped for hurting you like this."

Taken aback by the self-disgust in his tone, she gave him a teasing smile. "Well, you could always make it up to me."

He looked at her and gave her a slow smile that had her panties melting. "What do you have in mind?"

She swallowed hard, electric desire sparking between them and filling the small room like a storm. What she wanted to tell him was how badly she needed his cock inside her while he held her in his arms and made her scream with pleasure. Or how she wanted to drop to her knees and suck his dick, to use her hands and lips on him until he filled her mouth with his salty seed. She took a deep breath, trying to dispel some of her tension, but the scent of his cologne only made her more aroused.

She tried to tell him what she wanted, but here, in her living room, in such a normal setting, she didn't have the courage. Blast it, if she was still Dove, she could be as kinky as she wanted without shame, but here in her home she was Anya. And Anya was too shy to say those dirty things to Jesse in her brightly lit and entirely normal living room.

He gave her a bemused smile, and she realized she was taking too long with her answer. Flushing, she mumbled, "I don't know. Make me some chocolate chip cookies?"

He grinned and moved until only the smallest of spaces separated them, looming over her and making her aware of how much smaller she was than him. God, she wanted him inside her in the worst way but was too embarrassed to ask.

No, dammit. If she couldn't be strong for herself, she could be for Jesse. He'd demand nothing less, and she didn't want to disappoint her Master. "That's not the only place that hurts."

"I'm sorry, I—"

Gosh, she was horrible at trying to be seductive. She shook her head and tugged at his hand, leading him away from the bright living room to the dim shadows of her bedroom. Pausing, she looked over her shoulder at Jesse. "Let me show you what else you make ache on my body."

The flare of lust in his gaze almost brought her to her knees. She led him into her small bedroom, the pale silver and blue tones soothing her. The illumination from the open doorway gave her more than enough light to see by. Once they crossed the threshold, he pulled her against him and leaned down to claim her lips in a searing kiss that made her nipples draw into stiff points. He took his time, rousing her with nips of his teeth, strokes of his tongue, and his wonderful hands caressing her body until her blood boiled.

When he released her, they were both breathing hard and his erection pressed against the supple leather of his pants. "Show me where you hurt."

He moved past her and sat on the edge of her brass bed. He kicked off his boots and socks before reclining back on his elbows. She took a moment to admire him, to freeze the image of him in her bed into her mind. The pale blue comforter highlighted his body, and he gave her a grin filled with sensual promise. While disrobing for him had been so easy at the club, here in the sanctuary of her bedroom, it was almost impossible to get started. Here it felt real, like she was crossing some type of invisible line or opening Pandora's box. Once she took that first step, there was no going back.

Drawing in a deep breath, she tugged her T-shirt over her head and wished she'd worn something other than her plain white cotton panties and bra. But she hadn't been thinking when she left the club, her mind way too preoccupied to consider leaving on the sexy panties she'd made for her costume. His low rumble of approval at the sight of her breasts helped ease some of the tension within her. Good Lord, he'd seen her as exposed as a woman could be. Nothing she was revealing was anything new.

Unfortunately that knowledge didn't slow her speeding heart, and she wished as she pulled her pants down that she was skinnier, that her thighs didn't touch when she walked or her stomach pooch out when she sat.

She felt like with each layer of clothing she took off, she was exposing more of her true self, her soul to him.

Clad only in her bra and panties, she looked up at him through her lashes, drinking in the sight of all that masculine energy in human form, waiting for her. He was so big, so powerful. The fact he could hurt her badly if he wanted to but didn't aroused her and gave her the courage to approach him.

This was Jesse, her Jesse, her Master.

The clock next to her bed illuminated the side of his face with a cool blue glow, allowing her to see from the tightening of his jaw and flex of his arms that he wasn't as unaffected by her as he appeared to be. A tingling thrill ran through her and gave her the courage to allow the wanton side of her personality to come through. When she was close to him like this, immersed in him, everything else became secondary. She wanted to lose herself in him, needed to have all the bullshit of the day swept away by his strong will.

Glad she'd taken a quick shower at the club before she left, she watched him look her over slowly, his gaze drifting across her skin like a caress.

She reached out to touch him, but he grabbed her hand before it reached his face. "Go get the curtain ties from your windows."

Confused, she did as he asked, and returned with the long, silvery rope topped with navy blue tassels. After handing them to him, she stood next to the bed, unsure of what to do next. He seemed to sense her anxiety, because he moved so he was sitting on the edge of the bed with her cradled between his legs. Their height difference almost put their mouths level, and he ran his lips over her collarbone, pausing to lick the hollow of her throat.

"Put your arms behind your back, and lace your fingers together."

She did as he asked. He leaned closer, nuzzling the valley of her breasts while he tied her arms together behind her back. Instead of fastening the rope around her sore wrists, he tied her forearms together. This position caused her chest to thrust out, and with a harsh jerk, he pulled both cups down, making her exposed breasts wobble.

"Fuck. You have the prettiest tits I've ever seen."

Jesse leaned closer and began to lick a slow circle around her areola, a maddeningly unhurried pace that had her squirming.

He slapped her other breast, startling a gasp out of her. "Be still."

A groan stuck in her throat at the warmth now radiating through her stinging flesh. He returned to his oral assault of the other breast, his clever mouth and teeth scouring her body. When he bit down on her nipple, hard, her knees almost buckled, but he caught her about the waist, forcing her to stay pressed against him.

The tassels of the rope tickled across her bottom as his mouth went from one breast to the other, making her nipples ache and throb in the most delicious manner. When he'd driven her to the point of insanity, he gave each peak one more harsh nip, then pulled back, admiring his work.

"Nice. Almost red now instead of that pretty pink." He blew across her breast, making the abused tip crinkle.

She jerked at her bonds, wanting to touch him badly. "Master Jesse, please. Let me apologize for lying to you."

"You were a very naughty girl." He looked up at her, studying her face and making her feel terribly exposed and vulnerable yet still aroused. "I'm going to fuck your mouth, Anya, so next time you think about lying, you'll remember having to choke on my dick."

She groaned and stepped back so that he could stand. He took his shirt off and tossed it into the corner. He grabbed a pillow from the bed and tossed it to the floor at his feet. Before he could reach for his pants, she stepped forward, placing her lips on his chest, her mouth level with his nipple. She kissed him, trying to put into her touch how glad she was to have him here with her. That he hadn't fired her and more importantly that he still wanted to be with her despite her deception. If he wanted to empty himself in her mouth and leave her wanting, that was okay. She would do whatever he asked of her to try and make things right between them.

Working her lips down his body, pausing to lick at the edge of his ribs, over the sections of his hard abdominals, and finally down to his belly button, she stopped, unsure of how to get on her knees without losing her balance. As if sensing her dilemma, he helped lower her until her mouth was level with his crotch.

He opened his leathers and pulled them down enough to scoop out his erection and the heavy weight of his testicles. She licked her lips and went to take him into her mouth, but he grabbed a handful of her hair and held her still.

"No, Anya. This isn't about what you want to do. It's about what I want. Sit back on your heels and open your mouth as wide as you can."

She complied, and when the tip of his cock slid past her lips, over her tongue, and down her throat, she realized how very vulnerable this position made her. He held her still, his grip in her hair bordering on painful. In and out he slid, farther each time until she had to fight a gag when the fat crown of his head slipped into her throat.

Convulsively swallowing in an effort to take him deeper, she made him groan. "Relax your throat. Take me in, baby. You have no choice in the matter. I'm going to fuck your face, and you are going to be a good girl and take it."

Arousal spun through her until she thought she could almost feel his pleasure. She was so wrapped up in being what he wanted, what he needed, that she got a glimpse of what her compliance was doing for him. His powerful thighs rocked as he set an easy rhythm with his strokes. Precum slid over her tongue with each thrust, and her mouth watered, easing his passage. She was the one who was making him lose control. A heady sense of power and joy filled her with a warm tingle that only heightened her own arousal. Opening wider, she tried to swallow as much of him down as she could. Her Master was trusting her to give him pleasure, to obey his will, and she tried to show her obedience, her thanks, by making this the best blowjob he'd ever had in his life.

The only thing in her world was his scent, his taste, his flesh filling her.

He pulled out almost all the way. "Lick the head, then suck it."

Swirling her tongue over the fat mushroom cap, she then probed the slit, and he growled deep in his throat. Emboldened, she tried to lick farther into that small slit, to draw forth more of his liquid arousal. With a curse he jerked her head back, then slid himself in and out of her mouth, his pace becoming punishing. Tears prickled the corners of her eyes, her throat burned, and her arms ached from being bound behind her, but those discomforts only added to her arousal.

She'd endure all that and more for his pleasure.

He shoved himself all the way in until her nose was buried in his pubic hair, and held her there, making the air burn in her lungs as he filled her throat. One second passed, then another as the hot length of him throbbed between her lips. At last he pulled all the way out, and she took a gasping breath of air, her vision blurring with her tears.

He drew her up by her hair and turned her face so he could see her. "My beautiful girl, you did so well." He wiped her mouth, gathering the moisture from her lips, then rolled one of her abused nipples between his now slick fingers. "Someday I'm going to come down your throat, and you will suck every drop from me, but right now I have other things in mind."

Before she could ask what he meant, he pushed her down onto the mattress on her stomach so her legs hung off the edge of the bed. The comforter scraped across her sore nipples, and she turned her head to the side, the rasp of her harsh pants filling the room. He kicked her legs wider, then moved the panel of her panties over so that her pussy and ass were exposed.

"Should I fuck this pretty asshole?"

He pressed his finger against her puckered entrance, and a jolt of pure lust went through her. With his other hand he swept two fingers through her folds and brought the slick arousal to her anus. He then began to slowly massage the swollen tissue around her clitoris, forcing more blood to the area and further sensitizing her. Pressure was at her asshole again, but this time it was the gentle laving of his tongue, licking up her honey spread around that tight entrance. Good God, that felt so good, the alternating stimulation from his hands on her pussy to his mouth on her ass, his touch connecting the nerves of her body in the most pleasurable way ever.

He pulled his mouth away from her bottom, only to be replaced by one finger. He slid gently into her anus, and she groaned against the slight burn.

"Tilt your hips up and push back."

She did as he asked. The burning lessened and became an intense sensation that made her gasp. He began to slowly finger fuck her bottom, deliberate strokes that forced her to concentrate on every tiny bit of feeling. A second finger joined the first, pushing and probing against the tight ring of her anus before slipping in. He held his hand still, filling her, while he continued to massage her mound. Then he pinched her pussy lips, hard, over her clit and rolled the skin. She arched and shouted at the intense burst of ecstasy, pleasure detonating in her blood. He shoved a third finger in, and she tensed, the burning more than an annoyance now; it was a real pain. Making a soothing sound, he removed his fingers. Then he picked up his shirt from the floor and cleaned himself off.

"Hmm, not today."

She wiggled, wishing his finger was back pressing on that soreness, making her endure for his pleasure. "Please, Master. Take me any way you wish."

"Rest assured, Anya, you have no say in the matter. If I want to turn you over and fuck your tits, the only thing you'll be able to do is lick the head of my cock." He gave her ass a hard slap that made her cry out. "You do like your pain, don't you?"

Sinking into the warmth flowing through her, relaxing into the mattress, she moaned softly. "I like turning you on, Master."

He smacked her again, harder. "Be honest with me, Anya. Your sore nipples, your stinging ass, they all make your pussy wet, don't they?"

She nodded and earned another slap, this time where the sensitive skin of her bottom met her thigh. "Yes! It feels wonderful. Bad and good at the same time."

He leaned over, his weight crushing her back, his cock sliding between her ass cheeks. "When I do fuck you in that pretty, tight asshole, I don't think I'll stretch you too much first. I'll make your ass burn, make you cry, then make you come until the bed is soaked beneath you. There is something so sensual about licking the tears from a woman's cheeks as she comes hard around my cock. They won't be tears of pain but of release."

She shuddered, rubbing her butt against his dick as his words wove a magical dark spell around her. "Oh, please do that now."

He laughed, a rough chuckle that brushed across her skin. "You are so sweet, but I want that cunt clutching at me. I can feel it when I bottom out in you. Most women complain that it hurts, meaning I have to be careful, but you like it, don't you? I can fuck you as hard, as deep as I want, slam into your cervix, and it will only make you wetter, needier."

She nodded and clenched her hands, one big ball of craving for his dick.

"Say it."

"I-I love it when you fuck me until I ache."

"Hmm." He shifted so his cock pressed at her entrance. Her vagina contracted as if trying to suck him in. "I want you to walk around tomorrow sore. When we move you into your new room, I want to know you can still feel me between your legs. I enjoy knowing my submissive is wearing my touch on her body, even if it can only be felt, not seen. I bet when you press your thighs together tomorrow, you're still-swollen pussy will ache and get wet. Because I intend to fuck you hard tonight and again when we wake up."

All she could do was keen her need as he slowly breeched her entrance, sliding through her well-lubed passage but still having to fight her body. She tightened around him, enjoying his grunt as he had to use the muscles in his legs to push into her. With an endless stream of moans flowing from the pit of her belly and out of her throat, she clenched down as hard as she could.

"Goddammit, Anya." He pushed off and slapped her ass twice. "Open up for me. You aren't going to suck the cum out of me with that tight pussy yet."

He gave her a hard pinch on her butt, already burning from his slaps, and she gasped, her muscles relaxing and allowing him to slide all the way in. With a groan of his own, he picked her up by the hips, her toes barely scraping the floor. He was so strong, able to throw her around and use her body any way he wished.

It was such a fucking turn-on.

At first he kept his strokes slow and teasing, making her conscious of his every move. She begged him for more, harder, but he ignored her and continued the mind-blowing feeling of his dick moving in and out. Soon she fell into the rhythm, her bound arms and dangling legs making it impossible to do anything but feel. Then he slammed into her and hit deep, shoving hard against her cervix.

She screamed, and he stilled, his cockhead pressing inside her, no doubt anointing her stinging cervix with his precum. Her pussy throbbed around him, the desire spiking higher until she became mindless with it. But he continued to move in and out, taking her to the peak, then stopping, leaving her to clutch her inner muscles around him in a vain attempt to milk her orgasm out.

"God, little one, you are so tight, and your pussy is incredibly snug." He eased back out all the way and shoved in, driving another scream from her. "That's it. Take all of me. Every fucking inch." The last words were punctuated by him pulling out until the bulbous head of his cock stretched her entrance, to an incredibly long slide back until he bottomed out.

She turned her head to the bed, her tears soaking into the fabric as he hammered into her. Oh God, she hurt so good. He released her hips and grabbed her arms, forcing her body up into a curve, her breasts thrust out and shaking with his pounding. She drew nearer, tighter than the bow shape he'd put her in. He moved her forward until her clit rubbed against the edge of the bed with his thrusts.

"Oh, Master, please…"

"No, you don't come until I do."

He tightened his grip on her arms and lifted her higher. Her shoulders ached and her swollen clit pressed firmly against the mattress with each hard pounding. He was relentless, fucking her until her body screamed for its release.

"Come for me, Anya."

Three hard and deep strokes later, she did.

The tension in her body snapped, hurtling her down into the darkness where only pleasure and sensation existed. So fucking good, her body drank in everything he had to offer, the scent of his musk filling the air around her, saturating her with his presence inside and out. She tried to shove back at him, riding out her orgasm on his cock. He released her arms, his body shaking against hers as the first rush of semen blasted her abused womb. Together they rocked, his body crushing hers into the mattress as he leaned over to bite her neck hard.

That pain sparked a renewed contraction, and he groaned when she clamped down on him. Resting fully against her, his thighs still on hers, his twitching cock still buried within her, he began to whisper about how beautiful she was, how well she surrendered to him. Words that her soul drank down in a tone filled with such caring she couldn't help the renewed tears tracing down her cheeks.

Still inside of her, he untied her arms and massaged her shoulders. His gentle touch seemed to stroke her soul, and she loved that he was still connected to her, filling her with himself in a primal way that satisfied her completely. She wanted to stay like this forever, to never leave the comfort, the mind-numbing joy of being his.

Nothing mattered right now except her Master and his pleasure in her actions. She'd made him feel this way. Her and only her. She was his sweet, beautiful submissive. When he pulled out, she moaned in protest, but he hushed her.

He left her side, and she tried to slow her breathing, to

regain some semblance of control. Moving was beyond her right now. All she could do was sink deeper into the mattress until it felt like she was floating. A few moments later he exited the bathroom, and the vision of his now naked body walking toward her made her body tingle. She couldn't find the energy to move when he reached her side and pressed something blissfully warm and wet against her abused pussy.

At her moan he made a hushing noise. "Easy, little one. I'll take care of you."

After washing her, he patted her dry, then began to massage her shoulders again. Any bones she had left dissolved, and she was a lump of flesh on the bed, the enormous amount of endorphins and hormones his brutal loving had called from her body receding and leaving her feeling empty and washed-out. A shiver started somewhere deep within her and radiated outward.

He shifted her around the bed and managed to get her beneath the sheets with utterly no help on her part. Sliding in, he curled himself around her, surrounding her with his warmth. His heat filled the hollow space within, saturating her with his presence. Jesse was here, in her bedroom, holding her in his arms.

He was really here.

"Yes, Anya, I'm really here."

She didn't have the energy to blush. "I've dreamed about this."

He let out a pleased sigh, his breath tickling her ear. "When?"

"Since the first time I saw you smile."

He stiffened behind her; then his breath came out in a low rush that seemed to sweep across her soul. His hold gentled, became something more. She had to swallow hard, having never been held like this by anyone before. Like she mattered, like she was something special.

For a moment she wondered if he'd held his wife like this, then sent up a silent thank-you to Carol. Without a doubt she'd helped Jesse become the amazing man he was. He was someone who knew what it meant to love with his whole heart. She wondered if it scared him, but if his soft strokes of her body with his hands were any indication, he didn't seem too bothered by it.

Trying to turn off her overanalyzing brain, she sank into the moment. The feel of his body hair rubbing against her and the firm muscle beneath. His cologne and her perfume mixing together with the musk of sex. She'd come harder tonight than she even thought possible. She drifted, impossibly happy and content, cradled in his arms.

CHAPTER TWELVE

Something tickled Jesse's lips, and he absently tried to brush it away. To his right a female murmured, and he reached out, getting a handful of soft stomach and hip. It only took him a few seconds to remember. As soon as he did, blood rushed to his cock in a ball-tightening pound. Slowly opening his eyes, he looked around the dimly lit room.

Anya must have gotten up at some point because the door to her room was closed, and her curtains were pulled tight. Since this room faced to the west, it was still nice and dark. He looked over at the curvy woman and wanted to do bad things with her.

She slept like an innocent, one arm flung out to the side, her soft lips lightly parted. The golden spread of her hair around her body was indescribably sexy. He slowly shifted, wanting to get a better look at her body as she slept. Full, firm, and profoundly female, she was a work of art come to life.

He slowly drew the sheet covering her down, revealing inch by inch the rich cream of her skin. When the tips of her breasts peeked out, he grinned at the sight of his adoration. A bite mark shadowed the side of her breast, and her nipples were definitely darker than usual. And erect. The slide of the blanket over them must have reached her somewhere in her sleep, because she gave a sexy moan and shifted.

Pulling the sheet down farther, enjoying his submissive's body as was his prerogative, he drank in the way her ribs narrowed to the pleasing bump of her belly. It had felt so good to press her against him, all softness and warmth. At the first sight of her little cleft, he had to pull himself back. She was indeed swollen there as well. Not as puffy as she got while aroused but definitely pinker than usual. Poor girl. He was going to fuck her raw if he wasn't careful.

He really should make up for being such a cad.

Shifting on the bed, trying to disturb the mattress as little as possible, he drew the sheet entirely off her. When she made no move, he gently spread her thighs, exposing her to his gaze. He loved watching a woman's pussy become aroused, swollen, and wet. He leaned in and began to lick his way up through her slit, ending with a soft tap to her clit with his tongue.

She moaned and arched against him, earning a slow and gentle lick of her clit.

"Jesse..." She reached down and threaded her fingers through his hair. "Mmm, so good."

He loved how she kept her pussy completely bare of hair. Just licking over that delicate surface made her squirm. Returning his attention to her clit, he began to rhythmically suck on the hard bud, coaxing it fully out of the hood. Her moans became incoherent, little pleading noises that tightened his balls. Lapping at her with quick, methodical strokes, he drove her higher, noting the tension in her thighs.

Before she came, he pulled back and looked up. She was magnificent, her body arched, firm breasts shaking with her breath. All that beauty and warmth at his fingertips.

He pulled himself up the bed and swirled the head of his cock between her folds. She grabbed at him, trying to thrust her hips up, but he stopped her.

"Lift your head."

Her pretty blue-gray eyes clouded with confusion, but she complied. He adjusted her to the right height, mounding pillows behind her back before straddling her face. She immediately leaned up and began to tongue his balls with eager strokes. While she didn't have the skill that came from experience, her enthusiasm more than made up for it. Gripping the headboard, he moved so his cock bounced against her lips, his thighs pinning her arms down beside her. She immediately opened wide.

"Good girl." He slid his cock between her lips. "Take it all. Make me proud."

His words worked their magic, and she did as he commanded, her body obeying him without question. She struggled to take him in this position, but he didn't help her, too caught up in the fucking amazing sensation of her mouth. Like the rest of her it was small and tight, a tad too snug to comfortably fit his cock. He made sure not to rush it, let her adjust. His patience was rewarded when she swallowed around his dick. Holding himself there, not moving in and out was torture, but Anya seemed to like having her air cut off for a brief period.

Sure enough, when he pulled out, she took a deep breath and moaned hard enough to vibrate his balls. With a curse, he moved out of the silken trap of her mouth, wanting to fuck her, to be inside of her and make her come. He wanted her with a primal intensity that seared his bones, a need to possess.

He yanked her up by the waist, enjoying a deep kiss before he rolled them over so she was on top.

"I want you to ride me, little one. Grab me in your fist and put me in slow. I want to see you enjoy every inch."

Her breathing became labored, and he struggled to keep from slamming into her.

"Spread your pussy lips for me. I want to see the head going into your slick pink heat."

She did as he asked, and he growled at the sight of her cunt beginning to envelop his cock. At the first kiss of her soaked flesh, he clenched his teeth and returned his attention to her face in a vain effort to calm down. But when he saw the complete ecstasy in her expression, it only goaded him further into a bestial rutting state. Almost halfway down his cock now,

Anya made a little moaning noise that near killed him.

Knowing he was going to come if he didn't stop her, he smacked her hip.

"Stay right there. Do not move up or down my cock an inch. I want you to play with that pretty clit of yours until you orgasm, and only then can you take me all the way."

Her closed eyes tightened. "Master, I don't know if I can do that."

"You will do that, or I will pull out and come down your pretty throat instead of inside your cunt."

A slight whimper worked its way out of her mouth, but she reached between them and began to rub her clit with her thumb. He watched, fascinated with how she pleased herself, making notes as to how she touched and what she did. He'd been far too gentle with her clit. Watching her tug and roll that little nub made his cock throb.

His self-control was at the very edge, but he hardened his resolve. "Come on, baby. Make yourself come. Stroke that wet cunt of yours. Right now some of your honey is dripping down my cock, falling onto my balls. I'm going to make you clean it off."

She rubbed harder, faster until her thighs trembled with the effort of holding herself up. She tossed her head back, her hair a glorious waterfall of golden color. From this position he could actually see the blood flushing her sex, her clit hardening beneath her busy fingers as her orgasm approached. She froze, her thighs trembling, then came with a wail. Before her first wave had even crested, he slammed himself into her, the need to come making his balls ache.

She placed her hands on his chest, her hair falling in a curtain around them, and rode him hard. He helped her keep up the pace, rocking into her, pinning her down to grind her clit against his pelvis. He met her gaze, and the raw desire he saw there pierced his soul. He strengthened that connection, reaching out to her. It had been such a long time since he'd felt not...alone during sex. Everything low in his stomach gathered tight, and he grabbed handfuls of her ass, just rubbing her clit against him with his cock as far inside of her as he could get.

"Come again, Anya. Take me over with you."

"Master." The words passed through her lips in a breathy whisper.

"Look at me, Anya."

Opening her eyes, she gave him a sultry look that made his hips buck, losing his rhythm. She tightened until it felt almost like a fist gripping his dick. She let out a little whine, and he leaned up, catching her nipple between his teeth, and bit down. That pushed her over, and she cried out, calling his name in a ball-draining scream. He didn't even have to move, just stop holding his orgasm back. Without a single stroke her quivering pussy milked the sperm out of him, searing him with his release. Even as he came, even as the pleasure crested, he kept looking into her eyes.

Her beautiful blue-gray eyes.

He never wanted her to look at another man like this, ever. With their bodies still connected, contractions still shaking her and him, he decided he wasn't going to let her go without a fight. While he wouldn't stop her from going to Paris, he would imprint himself on her so fully no other man could take his place. He didn't give a fuck if she was too young for him, or if there would be snide comments about her having been his nanny. She was a good woman, and he would be a fool if he let her slip through his fingers. He'd brand himself into her soul, because she'd already put her mark on his.

He pulled her down to his chest, wrapping his arms around her small form, and began to plan.

—✦—

His mother looked up from where she sat reading a book to Mark. "Jesse, did you come home last night?"

Feeling ridiculous, he gave Mark a significant look. "Yes, Mom, I was out at the stables."

His mother flushed and mouthed the word *sorry* to him before sending Mark off to find Teddy and play with him. Once his son was out of sight, she turned back to him with a speculative gleam in her eye. "Did you spend another night at Isaac's or Hawk's house?"

He often played poker with the other men into the wee hours of the morning, so they would stay with whoever was hosting that night. Well, none of them really owned a traditional home, more like mansions and penthouses, but that was still the only times he stayed out all night.

Until now.

"Mom, it's kind of complicated, and I need your help."

She sat down on the couch and moved a toy out of the way before patting a spot next to her. "Jesse, come down here and tell me what is going on."

He sat with a heavy sigh and rubbed his hands over his face. Telling her was harder than he thought, and he chided himself for worrying his mother would lecture him for being attracted to Anya. "I'm falling in love with Anya, the nanny."

When his mother didn't say anything, he looked over at her, ready for the censure in her face. Instead her bright smile caught him off guard. "Anya?"

"Yes, Anya."

"Good."

"What?"

His mother patted his shoulder. "Honey, she's been making calf eyes at you for a long time now. You just didn't notice. I like her. She's a very smart and ambitious young woman."

"Mom, she's so young."

"Might I remind you that by the time I was twenty-three, you were already four years old?"

"But that's different." She laughed softly, and he avoided her knowing gaze. "Anya's my nanny. I don't want people thinking the wrong thing."

"What? That a handsome young widower fell in love with his beautiful nanny? Oh yes, that never happens. Besides, when did you ever care what other people thought?"

It amazed him that after all these years his mom could still put him in his place every time. "I don't want anyone to talk shit about her. Me, I *don't* care, but she's not used to being an object of gossip in the local paper."

"I know if I loved a man, I would put up with every paper in the world writing about us if it meant we could be together."

He shook his head. "Why did I come to a hopeless romantic to talk about relationships? What about Diane? Don't you think she'll have something to say about her sister's husband bringing another woman into her house?"

"Diane is a bitch no matter what." He blinked in surprise at the venomous tone of his mother's words. "She is only using her sister's death as an excuse to keep seeing you. The way she hits on you is pitiful. I'd be more worried if you noticed."

"What?"

His mind raced over the idea that Diane had hit on him. When she came over for her visits with the boys, they usually stayed here. Now that he thought about it, she'd never volunteered to have them over at her place. He'd thought it was because his house was equipped for kids while her condo in the city was filled with artwork that could easily be smashed to bits. Of course she'd also always urged him to stay and hang out with them, but usually he left them alone so they could have time with their aunt.

Plus he couldn't stand the woman.

His stomach clenched as he remembered her fleeting touches, things he'd excused as nothing because of course someone wouldn't hit on their deceased sister's husband. His flesh crawled, and anger filled him, but he couldn't stop the boys' visits. They were only five years old, and they loved their aunt, even if she was a self-centered bitch.

What a cluster fuck.

His mother waved her hand. "Never mind. We're not

talking about her. If she did say anything mean to or about Anya, I hope you will stand up for the woman whose opinion matters. And it's not that gold-digging peroxide-blonde bitch."

Stunned, he stared at his mother. He knew she didn't like Diane—hell, he didn't like her either because she'd been so cruel to Carol while they were growing up—but he didn't know his mom hated her. And his mother didn't hate easily. Her hands were clenched into tight fists in her lap, and it hurt his heart to see her so upset.

Covering her hands with one of his, he tried to catch her eye. "Don't worry. I would never let anyone hurt Anya."

"I know you won't. You're a good boy. Someone raised you right."

He laughed and released her hand. "That she did." He rubbed his face again, smelling Anya on his hands. "I wish things weren't so messed up with Anya. That I had met her somewhere else first."

"You like her. She likes you. What's the problem?"

"You know she's leaving for Paris in two weeks to spend the summer there."

"Ah, that's right." She unfolded her hands and leaned back on the couch. "A beautiful young lady alone in Paris for the first time. No wonder you're worried."

He grimaced at the mental image of Frenchmen trying to seduce his woman. "I don't want to ruin it for her. I want Anya to go to Paris and experience everything she can. I don't want to hold her back, but at the same time, a really selfish part of me wants to keep her here. To not give her an excuse to run."

"Have you talked with her about this?"

"Not yet. Things are...well, they were kinda complicated for a bit."

"I see. So what can I do to help you? I like Anya. She has a sweet soul, and the boys adore her."

"I know this is a big imposition, but I was wondering if you could help out with the boys for the next two weeks. I'm going to take some time off from work to spend it at home."

His mother laughed and patted his knee. "It's not called helping you with the boys. It's called being a grandparent. You know I have nothing to do since you moved me up here from Texas. I'd love to come and stay for a bit. If I don't come, I'll rot away in my apartment, watching reruns of *Judging Amy*, contemplating buying ten cats to dress up in doll's clothes."

"You're right. You would just sit there doing nothing. You have your business, your bridge club, your animal rescue group, Daughters of the American Revolution, your gardening club—"

"Those are all things to do. My grandchildren, my son, are more important than any of that. I don't like seeing you alone, Jesse. Like me, you're not one of those people who can go through life without a partner. I say go after Anya with both hands."

"I'm—uh—I asked her to take a spare bedroom in the house."

Her eyebrows flew up; then she managed to smooth her expression. "Thank God our bedrooms are on separate wings of the house."

"Gah, Mom, really?"

She rolled her eyes. "Mothers have sex too, you know."

He leaped off the couch and backed away. "Okay, seriously, if you never ever say that again, I'll send you on a cruise."

She laughed and shook her head. "Jesse, you have my blessings if that is what you're looking for. I'll help with the boys, and you can devote yourself to courting Anya. You have only two weeks to give her memories that will shine bright even when she's across the ocean in the City of Lights."

Chapter Thirteen

S o far, Anya's first day staying with Jesse and the boys in the main house hadn't gone quite like she expected. Case in point, the massive TV screen in front of her. Coated in butter.

Jesse shook his head, utter bewilderment on his face. "I still don't understand it. Teddy must have bent the laws of reality and space to do this in the time it took me to get Mark a drink from the kitchen."

She bit her lower lip, trying to keep from laughing. "Don't look at me. I was out with your mom at the bakery."

The memory of his mother pointing out the wedding cakes made her flush from the inside out. Jesse had told her his mother was aware of their situation, but he didn't tell her that his mother was ready to marry him off. On the drive to the bakery Anya had been peppered with questions about herself, her family, and her schooling. Oh, Jesse's mom had never been rude or pushy, just very...thorough.

Anya must have passed her test, because on the car ride home, Jesse's mother began to list his good qualities. For a while there she'd sounded like a used-car salesman. This was all moving really fast for Anya, and she wasn't sure how to handle it. She'd never been in a situation like this with a man before, let alone a man and his family.

Jesse's mom came back in with paper towels and bottle of spray cleaner. "I've got this. You two go say good night to the boys."

While Jesse turned right away to leave, Anya put her hand on his arm to stop him. "We can't leave your mom to clean this up alone."

His mother shook her head. "Out, both of you, now. I like doing things a certain way, and I don't want you two mucking up my work."

Jesse grinned and grabbed Anya's hand in his own. Her muscles melted, and a fire started in her belly. This was the first time today they'd been alone, and the desire that had slept, coiled low in her belly, stirred to life. His bare feet made almost no sound on the thick carpet, and he turned lamps down as they passed into the study, heading for the boys' rooms on the other side.

They said their good nights, and each boy gave her a big hug. The warmth of their affection clung to her, and when Jesse closed the door to Mark's bedroom, he smiled. She couldn't help but smile back.

He held out his hand, and she took it. "While they're a handful, they're so sweet they melt my heart."

"My mom used to say the cuter the baby, the bigger the trouble."

He laughed and closed the door to the study behind him. When he turned and met her gaze, her body flashed with pleasure, need burning through her veins. His brown eyes had gone dark, and something about his mannerisms changed. He became taller somehow, more imposing. When she realized he'd let the leash on his Dominant side slip, her arousal shot through the roof.

"I want you to go to my room, take a quick shower, and then present yourself naked on the bed."

"Um..." She chewed her lower lip, unsure if she was allowed to ask him questions.

"What is it, little one?"

"What do you mean by present?"

He smiled and released her hand, then took a step closer. "It means I want you kneeling on the bed with your thighs spread, your hands on your knees, and your head down. It's a beautiful position that allows me to admire you at my leisure. All of you."

She looked up at him, silently begging him to kiss her. He took no mercy, just holding her with his gaze. "Go, now."

As if his words had released her, she practically ran to his room. Once she had his door shut behind her, she stripped out of her clothes, throwing them over the pale wood floors and onto the heavy mission-style furniture. His bathroom was equally impressive, all shiny modern chrome and black marble. She took a quick shower but carefully cleaned every inch of her body. She wanted to be fresh for him so he could taste her all over.

After drying off, she clambered onto his big bed. She slid across the cream silk comforter to the middle, taking her hair down from the bun she'd put it up in while showering. It fell down her back, sticking to her still-damp skin. Her heart raced; she trembled with anticipation. Jesse's scent hung heavy in the air, and she breathed him in. Settling back more comfortably, she put her hands on her knees and began to wait.

She'd been sitting there for no more than a few minutes when the door to the bedroom opened. It shut with a soft *click*, and Jesse's deep rumble of approval tightened her nipples. He paused next to the bed and set some things on the side table. Metal clinked against something, and she wanted to look, but he'd told her not to, so she sat.

"Come here. Crawl to me."

She rose up onto all fours and tossed her head back, looking at him for the first time since he'd entered the room. He wore his dark brown leathers, and his chest was wonderfully bare. The thought of touching the deep reddish-brown fur over his tight muscles made her giddy with anticipation. He picked up a remote off the table and pressed a button, turning on the fireplace across the room. Another switch and the lights went out, leaving him illuminated by flames.

It was the right element for him, flickering golds and oranges that made his body glow. The bulge in his leathers caught her eye, and she licked her lips, imagining what it would be like to have him shove that big dick down her throat again. She became instantly wanton around him, easily slipping into her basest desires without a shred of embarrassment. Why should she be ashamed? He loved her reaction to him, and she loved everything about him.

Stopping before him, she sat back on her haunches again and spread her legs. His harsh exhalation thrilled her, and she arched her back, lifting her breasts for him to enjoy.

"Why, Anya, you are wet. Have you been touching yourself?"

"No, Master. I'm wet because I've been waiting for you."

"Such a sweet girl." He palmed her breasts, rubbing his thumbs gently over her nipples. "Unfortunately while I will be eating that pussy tonight, I won't be fucking it."

She frowned up at him. "Master? Why not?"

"Because I'm going to fuck your ass instead."

She closed her eyes, overwhelmed by the sensual threat of his words. God, what would it be like to have that burning in her bottom from being stretched around his long cock? Would it feel better for him? Would she be able to endure the pain for his pleasure?

"But first, I have something I think you'll love."

She shivered in anticipation when he pushed her back, spreading her legs wide. Kneeling next to the bed, he spread the lips of her pussy and licked her. Just like that, her desire became painful, an ache to come, a tensing of the muscles that would only get worse. He pulled away and grabbed a small vial off the table. Opening it, he dropped a single bead onto her mound, then capped the bottle.

The cool liquid slid down to her slit, where his tongue

caught it. He spread the oil around her clit, focusing only on that little bundle of nerves. He worked her so well, teasing and arousing until her heels dug into the mattress and her hands fisted the sheets. Damn, he was going to make her come from sucking on her clit.

Right before it pushed her over the edge, he pulled back, causing her to cry out at the loss of his mouth.

"Wait," he said against her sex. The warmth of his breath made her clit feel like it was on fire.

"Oh God! It burns!"

"Yes, it does." He gave an evil laugh that went well with the burning torment between her legs. "You are going to become so sensitized a wisp of silk over your poor clit is going to be too much."

She groaned, unable to form words, and he massaged the nub. Holding his thumb against the tip, he pushed the little hood back, fully exposing her to his touch. He began to pinch and pull her clit, her hips jerking in response to his touch. He stood and pressed on her lower stomach with his free hand, making her endure his touch, feel the painful fire morph into bone-clenching need.

"Fuck!"

"Such language. Flip over on your stomach and put your ass up into the air."

Only too eager to do something that would give her relief, she did as he asked.

"Higher. Push that ass out."

Whimpering, she arched farther and groaned when oil poured over her puckered entrance. His fingers followed, pushing the oil into her bottom. Thankfully the lubricant he used on her bottom didn't burn. She whined at the stretch, at the ache that slid down to her clit and rebounded to her ass, creating a loop of sensation that had her thrusting against his fingers. He added a third, and she shook, on the edge of orgasm.

"Go over, baby. I've got you."

With that he reached down and lightly slapped her clit, giving her exactly what she needed to come. She moaned into the blanket, a long, intense release melting through her bones. It was the kind of release that made her slowly wiggle, feeling so good and relaxing. Through it all he continued to stroke her ass.

"Good girl. Now crawl up the bed until you reach the headboard."

She eagerly complied, the bed dipping when he joined her a moment later, now deliciously naked. His shadow filled the wall before her, looming over her in dim light of the fire. She reached the top and paused, waiting for him, the pulsing bundle of nerves that was her clit once again hardening under the relentless stimulation of the oil. He reached over her and wrapped a leather cuff first around one wrist and tied it to the headboard, and then the other. It forced her to hold on to the headboard, not giving her enough slack to lie down.

Effectively trapped, she tugged at the bonds and melted a little more at the realization he'd left enough slack in the cuffs that she could slip out if she wanted to. The knowledge that she was a willing captive made it all the more delicious for her.

Leaning over, he whispered into her ear, "You once said you liked to be trapped, forced to do things. Well, I have you imprisoned now, and no matter how much you beg, cry, or plead, I'm going to fuck that tight little ass of yours." He placed a kiss on her banging pulse. "If you are in true pain, the kind that you can't endure, use your safe word, ivy, and I'll ease off. If you want to play into it, get into the role of reluctant damsel, I have no problem playing back. Trust me when I say having you at my mercy is a turn-on. So feel free to say no and protest all you want. Unless you say ivy, I'm not stopping."

His warmth left her, and she startled a moment later when his brisk hand came down hard on her ass. "I'm going to beat you until I'm satisfied, and there is nothing you can do about it."

She moaned, low and deep, clutching the wood of the

headboard. True to his word, he rained blows down on her bottom, working her over until every inch of her skin seemed to vibrate. He rubbed his hands over her burning cheeks, then slapped both palms hard on her ass.

She yelped. "That hurt!"

"Good. I want it to hurt. I want it to burn for you, Anya. Because you are a bit of a pain slut, I bet your pussy is dripping wet right now." He shoved his hand between her legs, easily sliding his fingers into her swollen sex. "Feel that? Nice and hot for me."

"No, I don't like it."

He began to finger fuck her, and she moaned, rocking on his hand, showing her words to be a lie. Well, she didn't really like it; she loved it. Hadn't she always liked some pain with her sex? Even if it was just biting her lip until it bled, she would always do something to give that bit of added spice her body craved.

"You do like this, but you won't like what I'm about to do."

He leaned back; then the blunt head of his cock pushed against her asshole. She immediately clenched and earned a harsh slap. "Open up, Anya, or I swear I will fuck you until your voice is gone but not let you come. Now open that pretty ass for me and push back on my cock. I want you to fill yourself with me. I want my good girl to make herself hurt for my pleasure."

Trying to relax, she pushed back, conscious of the soft sounds of encouragement he made. Each tiny inch set her on fire inside, a burn that truly hurt. He was so big, so long that by the time she had him almost all the way inside, her body was slicked with sweat. A sense of pride mixed with her desire, a warm glow that made her work all the harder for him. She wanted to be everything he'd ever wanted in a submissive, because he was everything she'd ever wanted in a man.

"Fuck, you're tight. But this will make you even tighter."

Before she could wonder what he meant, he slammed his

dick in the rest of the way, and she screamed. He ran soothing hands down her back, over her abused bottom, and across her throbbing clit. "Shh, you can take it. You can cry if you want, but you will take it." He massaged her shoulders, then down her back, his touch calming even as his dick was a shaft of burning pain inside her.

A moment later something pushed at the entrance to her pussy, and she shuddered.

"It's a vibrator, Anya. Not too big. This should help you get past the discomfort."

He grunted and started to slide his dick out as he pushed the toy into her. What felt like an enormous cock in her pussy came to life, vibrating against her G-spot. A switch flipped in her head, and when he slammed his dick back into her, she yelled, this time with pleasure.

He was so fucking dirty, she loved it. Every time he went balls-deep, he would shove the vibrator hard into her wet pussy. All too soon she began to tremble with the need to come. He slowed his strokes but leaned down over her body.

"Come as much as you want, Anya." He pressed deeper, making her burn, and reached around to fondle her clit. "In fact, come right now, with your ass stuffed full of my dick."

She almost lost her grip on the headboard when the first wave hit, sweeping over her and pulling her out to the warm depths. He began to fuck her harder, no longer holding back, using her orgasm as an excuse to move like he wanted. The vibrator continued to hum, making her twitch and jerk as her release was never really allowed to end.

"Jesse, Master...oh, thank you." She pushed back at him, meeting his thrusts.

His gripped her hips and changed his angle, stretching her in a new way. "Your pretty little asshole is close to tearing, all snug around my cock. We'll have to make sure you wear a butt plug before we do this again." His words came out strained, and she threw her hair back, looking over her shoulder at him.

His gaze was fixed on where his cock was going in and out of her body, the firm line of his jaw clenched and a light smattering of sweat on his chest. The shadowed ridges of his abdominals flexed and contracted with each thrust, driving her crazy. All too soon she began to feel the tension returning, and she abandoned herself to it, losing her mind in the rough vortex of desire Jesse pulled from her.

Her next orgasm came when he pinched and rolled her nipples while jabbing at her with short strokes. The one after that from another round of spanks, and then a third from him rubbing her clit. By the end of the last one, she was barely holding on to the headboard.

He withdrew long enough to unhook her from the headboard before throwing her onto her back. With a low snarl he spread her legs and placed her ankles over his shoulders.

"Tilt your hips. Lift them up for me."

She did and whimpered when his cockhead pushed against her sensitive anus. When he slid in, she had to grit her teeth against the pain. He must have seen her discomfort because he went slow, then began to move the vibrator in and out of her pussy. He looked feral, almost savage as he focused on where their bodies joined.

He slid in, the vibrator out, over and over again until it almost felt like she was being fucked by two cocks. Despite being worn-out to the point of fainting, her hips snapped up to meet his thrust, her body craving another orgasm. The greed she had for Jesse bordered on compulsion, but she was helpless to resist him. He wanted another orgasm from her, and she wanted to give it to him.

He rammed into her now, the bed shaking with his thrusts. Each blow drew a cry from her until the room filled with her constant short screams. His dick swelled in her ass. She forced herself to look at him. Fuck, he was magnificent, about to come, his muscles locked solid and a fierce twist to his mouth.

With his head thrown back, he fucked her with abandon,

taking his pleasure from her willing and abused flesh. She looked down, watching her clit brush his groin, a swollen bud of pink against his fur. Gripping him hard with her ass, she earned a low groan, and he looked down at her.

"My Anya."

Intense emotions of joy and contentment flowed through her at the tenderness of his words, a sharp contrast to the punishing way he was using her. When he tugged hard on her clit, she spasmed, the pleasure too much. Ignoring her cries, he continued to tug at her until her ass and cunt clamped down, delicious shivers of desire mixing with an intense rush of endorphins that blindsided her. She froze against him, but he thrust in a half dozen more times, his breath ragged before he gripped her ass hard enough to bruise.

"Coming. Oh fuck yeah. So fucking good."

Knowing her Master was coming gave her the edge she needed for her own orgasm to roll through her, a slow rush that swept her away. His cock pulsed inside of her, bathing her with his seed, a soothing balm against her skin. Over and over he said her name, slowing his strokes. When he pulled out the vibrator and turned it off before tossing it on the bed, she cried out. And then he began to slowly pull his semihard shaft from her bottom, a stinging burn making her cringe.

"Hold on, baby. I'm going to go draw a bath for us. I'll be right back."

She curled up on her side, her lower half throbbing with the beat of her heart. One moment she hurt; the next she felt like she was sinking into the mattress again. When he picked her up, she offered no resistance, only smiling dreamily up at him as he told her how well she'd served him, how brave she'd been, how special she was to him.

The heat of the water licked at her as he sank them down into the tub. When the water touched her roughly used anus, she yelped and tried to struggle away, the sleepy feeling gone as her butt stung and burned.

"Shh, it's okay. I've put a special kind of bath salt in the tub that will soothe you. Give it a chance to work."

"Ow," she complained as he turned her so her back lay against his front. "It stings!"

"Easy, baby. Just breathe. Let it pass."

He slowly stroked his fingertips up and down her arms beneath the water, a soothing touch that had her relaxing inch by inch. Soon her body quieted, and her mind was content to drift, no real thoughts intruding, only living in the moment. She felt so connected to him and reveled in the sensation of her sore bottom, proof she'd served him well.

"Go ahead and fall asleep, Anya. I've got you." He wrapped one arm around her waist.

She let out a long sigh and stretched before curling into a more comfortable position with her cheek pillowed on his chest. His heart beat sure and steady, a dim thunder that blended in with her own. The warm water cradled them, and when he began to stroke her hair, she wondered how she would ever have the strength to leave him.

CHAPTER FOURTEEN

Jesse leaned against the counter of his kitchen and watched Anya and his mother doing the dishes while they talked about a sewing machine in rapturous voices usually reserved for women talking about diamonds. Growing up, his mother had made his clothes—cheaper than buying them—and he'd never realized how much work she'd put into it. Listening to her now talk about staying up late after he was off to bed to finish a new pair of pants for her ever-growing boy made his love for her tighten his chest.

Anya looked beautiful tonight. She wore her long blonde hair in a braid that swung around her back as she moved. Instead of her usual sweats, she wore a pair of jeans that cupped her ass in a way that made his hands twitch to grab a handful. While her pale blue flannel shirt wasn't sexy in the traditional sense, he enjoyed how it hugged her breasts. Plus the color brought out the natural pink in her lips and cheeks. She was the kind of girl all the guys would have been drooling over back home in Texas.

Fresh-faced, curvy body, and sweet as sugar.

Mark and Teddy were busy playing with watercolors at the kitchen table behind him. He'd go back and help them work on their paintings in a few minutes. Right now he wanted to watch the two women he cared the most about. The last few days had passed by in a blur of passion, warmth, and laughter. It had been a long time since his home had been filled up with so much feminine joy.

The doorbell rang, and both women looked up, catching him staring. Anya flushed and gave him a shy smile while his mother's knowing smirk made his cheeks want to heat. Clearing his throat, he stood and brushed some imaginary lint off his jeans. "I'll go get it. Don't leave for the ice cream parlor without me."

At the mention of ice cream, the boys abandoned their painting and swarmed the women, each excitedly chattering about what kind of treats they wanted. Anya gave him an exasperated look, and he chuckled. Rolling her eyes, she picked up Teddy and sat him on the edge of the counter, listening to his chatter while she rinsed dishes from dinner.

Jesse left the kitchen with a deep contentment settling into his bones. Thoughts of Anya leaving all too soon tried to intrude on his thoughts, but he pushed them away. Every day with her was a gift, and he wasn't going to waste it on the what-ifs.

He reached the foyer and flicked on the light before opening the door. His good mood headed south in a hurry when he found his former sister-in-law, Diane, beaming at him from the other side. For a moment he really looked at her, made himself see her.

Tonight she wore a pair of black high heels and a short green sweater dress that clung to her lean figure. His wife had been a runway model before they met, something her sister, Diane, had also done. While Carol had left the fashion world behind when they married, Diane had continued to model. Now she was dressed like she was going to a fancy party instead of playing with her nephews. Her long fingernails made it impossible to do things like puzzles with them, and she could hardly walk let alone run in those high heels. It was obvious she'd dressed to flirt, not to play with her nephews.

Diane preened beneath his gaze, and he realized with a start that she thought he was admiring her. His mother's words came rushing back to him. He frowned at the other woman.

"What's up, Diane? I thought you were coming over

tomorrow. You should have called first."

Her smile faltered at his cold tones. "Well, I didn't know I needed to call before visiting my nephews."

"But it would have been nice if you had."

She frowned at him, the lines around her mouth deepening. "Next time I will. I didn't know I had to call before I came to visit *my* family."

A pinprick of guilt jabbed at him, and he wished she'd leave and stop fucking up what had been a wonderful day. "We were about to go to the ice cream parlor."

"Oh, I'd love to come." She gave him a dazzling smile as fake as her tits.

"I'm sorry, but our car is full."

She blinked at him and took a step closer. "Who are you taking with you?"

"My girlfriend."

The whites of her eyes showed as she stared at him. "You have a girlfriend?"

As if on cue Anya entered the foyer with a wide smile. "Jesse, we're almost ready to go." She came up next to him and slipped her arm through his in a proprietary manner. "Hi, Diane."

Diane gaped at her; then her gaze narrowed until her eyes were angry slits. "You're sleeping with the help?"

Jesse moved Anya to his side but didn't let go of her hand. "No, I'm falling in love with a woman that is everything you aren't. Kind, generous, and beautiful inside and out."

Changing tactics, Diane's expression went from vicious to sorrowful so fast it was almost funny. "How could you do this to my sister? How could you bring another woman into her home?"

Resisting the urge to slap her, he took a deep breath and drew comfort from Anya's presence. "Fuck you, Diane. Your sister would love Anya."

Anya stepped in front of him and crossed her arms. "You

will not raise a scene like this with children in the house."

"Slut," Diane hissed.

Anya laughed. "I've been called worse by better."

It amused him to see Diane struggling to figure that out, but Anya was right. He couldn't argue like this where his boys could hear her shrieks. Fuck, they probably heard her bitching all the way down to the river. He moved Anya away from the door again and tried not to smile at the hostile looks she gave Diane. Who knew his sweet, innocent Anya could get so scrappy when she was riled up.

"Diane. Go home. You should be ashamed at using Carol's memory to try and guilt me. You should also be ashamed for attacking Anya. She has done nothing to you." He blew a harsh breath out of his nose. "What is wrong with you? I thought you were better than this, but I guess you're still the same girl that made Carol's life hell at home."

Tears glimmered in Diane's eyes, and he wasn't sure if they were real or fake. "Fine, I see how it is. Enjoy screwing someone young enough to be your daughter."

She turned on her heel, then stomped down the walkway to where her Mercedes sat gleaming in the night. After closing the door, he rolled his neck to try and release some of the tension. Anya leaned against the wall near the front door, looking out the window with a glare.

"I'm sorry you had to see that, baby."

She looked over at him, then back at the window. "She is such a bitch, but thanks for standing up for me."

Moving away from the window, she wrapped her arms around him and hugged him tight. He placed his lips on the fine silk of her hair, breathing in her scent. God, he felt so good when he was with her. His addiction to her could only result in pain when she left, but he couldn't tear himself away.

"Your mom sent me to the rescue," she muttered against his chest.

Hugging him seemed to be one of her defense mechanisms. She found solace in his arms and liked to close her eyes and be held when she was upset. It moved him in a profound way. Being needed was one of the best things about being a Dom, at least for him. He gained a sense of satisfaction like no other from being able to be everything his sub needed.

Her happiness was his happiness.

The joy and warmth in his body expanded until he became overwhelmed by the sensation and realized he loved Anya.

Truly loved her.

The heart worked in mysterious ways, and fate could be a real bitch.

Stepping back, he tilted her head up and grinned. "So, you came to rescue me from that bitch?"

She flushed, the pink rising to her cheeks and giving her an adorable warmth. "Something like that."

"Well, I'm glad you did." He brushed back some hair from her cheek, stroking her oh so soft skin. "That had been a long time coming, and I'm sorry you got caught up in the crossfire, but thank you for being there for me. You are an amazing woman."

She smiled up at him, pure devotion and happiness radiating from her. God, she was sweet. Unable to help himself, he pulled her around the corner into the unlit den. She giggled and tugged at him in a futile attempt to get away. Throwing her onto the wide couch, he pinned her with his knee and fished his phone out of his back pocket.

Anya tried to squirm away, but he then straddled her, and she was stuck.

He dialed his mom's number, and she picked up right away. "Jesse? Why are you calling me from the house?"

"Mom, I need you to take the boys out for ice cream, please."

Anya protested, and he put his free hand over her mouth.

His mother laughed. "Of course. The boys are ready to go. I think I'll stop by my place and make sure my plants are watered. Want us to bring you back anything from the parlor?"

He lifted his hand from Anya's mouth. "What kind of ice cream do you want?"

"Strawberry."

He nodded and put his hand back over her mouth, earning an outraged and muffled complaint. "Bring us back some strawberry and pralines and cream, please."

"Got it."

"Night, Mom."

Before she could respond with some suggestion about how he could sweep Anya off her feet, he hung up and tossed the phone onto the table. Moonlight glinted off the modern chrome lamps on either side of the couch and lovingly caressed Anya's lush curves. She raised her eyebrows, but he didn't release his hand. With a muffled sigh she settled down, already familiar with his tendency to like looking at her.

He'd explained to her that once he was rising into his Dominant headspace, he noticed things that normally slipped past his attention. Like the faint shimmer of some kind of glittery eye shadow she'd used to make her eyes look bigger, or the tender curve of her earlobe. The more he focused on her, the less the real world mattered. She became the center of his universe, a bright star he could touch without being burned.

Tonight he was the one who ached, who couldn't wait to be inside her. After all the times he'd had her, he should have been over the initial rush of taking a sub, but even now he wanted to rut on her like a beast in heat. An idea came to him, an answer to a problem he'd been mulling over the last few days.

When he at last removed his hand, she kissed his palm and smiled up at him. "Hi, Master."

"Hello, little one."

She bit her lower lip and looked up at him through her lashes. Minx. She knew exactly how to get him going. "What are you going to do with me, Master?"

"We're going to play a game."

"Will Master share with his most humble submissive the nature of the game?"

He smiled and moved off her before drawing her to her feet. "We're going to play hunt the subbie." He smiled at her, and her eyes went wide. Good, she was catching on to his mood. "I'm going to give you one minute to go hide somewhere in the house. If I find you and capture you within five minutes, I get to tie you to a chair, cover you in vibrating things, and go watch some TV."

"Hey, that's not fair!"

He gave her butt a hard pinch. "Well, I can't really punish you by beating you. The pain turns you on too much, and I could never really hurt you." He stroked his hand over her cheek, the soft down of her skin entrancing him. "And I can't threaten you with fucking you hard because you love it when you can't walk the next morning."

She gave a sound that reminded him of a satisfied purr. "Mmm, you're right as always, Master. I love wearing your mark on my body, in my body. It makes me feel like you're with me wherever I go." She stood on her tiptoes and placed a kiss on his chin. "What do I get if I win?"

"A surprise."

His own heart thudded, and she cocked her head at him, looking closer. Not wanting to give anything away, he spun her around and held her to his chest. "One."

"Wait, are we starting?"

"Two."

"No, hold on. I wasn't—"

"Three."

Before he got to four, she ducked out of his arms and ran, her braid flying behind her. He couldn't help but growl at the way her ass and tits bounced when she ran. She looked so...lush. Delicious. And she had the pinkest little pussy he'd ever seen. Made him want to do wicked things to her.

The seconds ticked by, and he listened for the sound of her footsteps, a creak somewhere that would tell him where she'd gone. At the count of sixty he looked at his watch, marking his five minutes for finding her. He really didn't want her to lose, but damned if he could stop his competitive side. She would get what was coming to her one way or another tonight.

A cursory scan of the kitchen revealed nothing, and he went on to the living room. She wasn't behind any curtains or under any pieces of furniture. He kept his search methodical, room by room, examining everything. After he'd exhausted the first floor, he sprinted up the stairs to the second level. He had less than a minute to spare.

Instinct had him dashing for his bedroom, and he made it at four minutes and fifty-nine seconds. Technically under the five-minute mark. He didn't have to look hard. She was kneeling next to his bed, her head down and legs spread. At some point she'd put a glittering gold chain around her waist. It was thick enough that he could hold on to it while he fucked her from behind, so he could really spear her on his dick.

His whole body clenched, and a deep-seated need to claim her tried to hurry him across the room. He looked away from her pussy, so bare and smooth, and back to her face. She peeked up at him through her lashes and gave him a mysterious smile. His balls drew up tight. He almost didn't want to touch her. She looked so beautiful, perfectly poised, awaiting his pleasure.

Gritting his teeth, he prepared to give her what she needed to come. A little pain. That was her own personal spice. While he'd never get off on really hurting her—the very thought made him ill—fulfilling her needs stroked him in a whole different way. And if he was an honest man, he also had to admit he found it fucking hot. To see her straining to take his length, the soft cry just for him as she came...it was his spice of choice.

"On your knees, darlin'. I'm in the mood for you to worship me."

Her lips pressed together as she tried not to smile. "Whatever my Master wishes."

He strolled over to the table next to his bed and picked up the remote for the stereo system. After pushing a button, a deep, sensual rush of music poured over them. It set the tone, the mood, and enhanced his pleasure in her. The music had a soulful side, almost melancholy, and he wondered if she felt that as well. Her breath hitched as he held her gaze, and he motioned to her by curling one finger.

"Your Master wishes for you to get over here and undress me."

She crawled across the floor to him, a slinky movement that never failed to make his cock jump. Anya was so observant; she remembered what he liked and tried to please him at every turn. That only made him want her more and to make it as good for her as he could. He'd planned a little something earlier in the afternoon, a setup that would allow her to watch herself getting fucked by him.

Her deft touch stroked over him, and he took a deep breath of her flowery scent, a mixture of delicate perfume and woman. He indulged himself in running his hand through her hair while she unbuttoned his shirt.

So pretty, like sun-bleached wheat.

Next she went to her knees and undid his pants. He stepped out of them, and she carefully folded them before putting them on his dresser. The sway of her walk was enough to bring any man to their knees, him included. When she returned, the view was even better. The moment she got close enough, he grabbed her tits, hard.

"I'm going to bind these tonight."

She shivered against him, the dreamy look coming into her eyes that was her physical sign for starting to drift down into her subspace. Sometimes his girl was in the mood for it rough and nasty—well, most of the time—but he also liked to make love to her.

Except he liked to make love with ropes and clamps.

"Follow me, Anya."

He took her into his closet and shut the door. After flicking the lights on, he went to the wooden shelves that held his shoes and pressed a hidden button. The shelves became a door, with only darkness showing from the other side.

Anya gaped at him. "You have a secret closet in your closet."

He couldn't help but laugh. "Not quite. Follow me."

Groping around in the darkness, he found his lighter and the candle he'd placed here earlier. To say this was his closet wasn't quite true. It was actually what used to be a small servant's room off to the side. When he'd bought the home, he'd converted it to be his dungeon. After his wife's death, he couldn't bear to go in there, the memories too strong. Then he met Anya, previously known as Dove, and he'd gone into the room and begun to clear it out. His friends Isaac and Hawk had come over, helping him remove the now dust-covered and neglected BDSM equipment. When there was nothing but the walls, the stained glass, and the bare wood floors, he'd cleaned every inch of it. In doing so it almost felt like he'd been cleaning a part of his soul, a place that had gotten as dusty as this room.

He'd never had a woman back here except for his wife. But now he had Anya, even if only for a brief time. He'd be a fool not to let her light into this place of shadows.

She gave a small gasp and turned in a circle, looking at the blue and green stained glass window. "I always wondered where this room was. I could see it from the outside, but I could never figure out where the door was inside the house."

The room was almost bare at the moment, just black silk walls and a gleaming oak floor. It was dark, hard to see outside of the circle of light from the candle, so he led her deeper into the room where his surprise waited. When it came into view, Anya stopped.

"Oh my."

He'd brought a foam mattress pad in here and covered it

with black silk. An antique Chinese medicine cabinet stood off to one side with pillows mounded against it for a headrest. He moved closer to the bed, lighting a few more candles until their reflections blazed back at them from the five big mirrors he'd brought in here.

Each had been positioned so they could watch each other from pretty much any angle they wanted. He wished he could make a video with her, but as fucked-up as the world was today, he knew something like that would never be safe. So instead he'd burn this into his memory, a vision to comfort him when her scent had faded from his sheets and she was an ocean away.

"Master, Jesse, this is just amazing. I can't believe I never found it. Not that I was in this wing of the house much anyways."

He continued to watch her, entranced by her naked beauty and honesty. "Did you ever want to sneak into my room? See where I slept? Smell my pillow."

She flushed scarlet from her chest to her hairline. "No."

"Really? You're not lying to me, are you? We both know what happens to girls that lie."

Her voice came out husky, similar to the sexy voice she used while pretending to be Dove. "They get punished."

"Get on the mattress and present yourself."

She practically skipped across the room. He had to hide an amused smile. Then she crawled forward, and the elongated almond shape of her pink pussy between her creamy thighs made his dick jerk. He could eat her pussy for days and still want more. She was so sweet and fresh tasting, and he could never get enough of the way she unraveled for him during an orgasm.

Once Anya was in the kneeling position, he went over to the medicine cabinet and brought out the black silk rope and grabbed a vial of oil. He could actually see her pussy clench at the sight of the ropes as he walked over to her, her widespread stance revealing her every aroused move.

He ran the rope through his hands, enjoying the way her gaze followed his fingers. "Put your hands behind your head."

Kneeling next to her, it was torture to not just fuck her right then and there. He began to wind the rope around her back, around both of her breasts, and then back around again. The contrast of white skin, black rope, and pink nipples that would only get bigger as he played, and the scent of her pussy were an artwork all their own. To him there was nothing more beautiful than this.

He finished the twist, securing her breasts. Before cinching for the final time, he ran his fingers around the rope pressing her tits together, trying to judge how tight they'd get. Knowing how much Anya liked it rough, he was afraid she'd try to take on too much her first time. It would be better to give her a little room to adjust. Besides, the clamps he was about to put on those pretty tits were harsh enough on their own.

He leaned forward and slowly licked over the tip of Anya's nipple, little teasing strokes that made her hips twitch. There was a certain pleasure to warming her up slowly, and he wanted to savor it. Switching to the other breast, he repeated the teasing motion and scratched his beard against the tip.

She mewled but didn't pull away.

He stood and returned to the medicine cabinet, pulling out some golden chains with tweezer clamps on two of the ends, and a smaller one designed for her clit. They'd only played with nipple clamps a little bit, but he'd enjoyed her reaction. So much that he'd order this pair for her from a renowned jewelry maker who also made BDSM implements. The gold was real, as were the diamonds hanging from each clamp, small bursts of light that glittered like stars.

She maintained her position, but when he brushed the tip of her breast with the clamp, she gasped. "Oh, Master. Those are beautiful."

"They're only decoration for the real beauty."

She smiled at him; then her eyes widened as he applied the clamps. For a moment the arousal dimmed in her gaze, so he played with the trapped nipple a little bit, coaxing her back into losing herself in the sensation. When he finally took them off, she'd be so fucking aroused it wouldn't even matter.

After the second clamp was put onto her hard nub, he leaned forward and gave her nipple a lick. She gasped, and her hands fell to his back. "Oh God."

With her breasts bound, her nipples clamped, her chest would soon become very sensitive. He brushed his beard over first one nipple and then the other, making her little hands claw at his back. While she was distracted, he picked up the dangling third rope, attached to the other two by a gold ring studded with pavé diamonds. He flicked his tongue against her nipple while parting her labia with one hand and seeking her clit with the other. The pretty bud was already hard, so it was easy to slip the clit clamp in place.

Her immediate scream, then harsh moan as he put two fingers into her eager cunt, made him smile. He rose higher on his knees, still finger fucking her while she neared her climax. Lucky for him she was the kind of woman who could be coaxed into three or four orgasms before she was done. Continuing to finger her, he fisted her hair and titled her head to his mouth.

She immediately opened for him, and their tongues stroked against each other. He rubbed the heel of his palm over her mound. That was all it took to make her come. She tried to fight it, bless her heart, but she stood no chance. Besides, he wanted an excuse to punish her.

As her pussy sucked at his fingers with her strong contractions, he stopped kissing her and shook his head. "Naughty girl. You're going to have to pay for coming without permission. On your back."

With a dazed look, she did as he said, her bound breasts flushed and growing tighter.

Perfect for fucking.

Grabbing the vial of grape-seed oil he'd brought over earlier, he lubed his cock up until it was dripping liquid onto her stomach. Straddling her waist, he grabbed her tits with both hands and looked down at her. She whimpered at his touch, and her eyes were closed, allowing him to inspect her at his leisure. He began to slowly push his cock between her bound breasts, the feeling almost like sliding into a pussy.

One of the blessings of having a long dick was that he could titty fuck a girl and get a blowjob at the same time. When the mushroom head of his cock brushed her chin, Anya opened like a good submissive and sucked at the head of his dick with an eager moan. He sat down a little firmer on her, the ring connecting the chains to her clit and nipples beneath him. Tears began to spill from her closed eyes even as pleasure suffused her face. Pulling back, he made sure to drag the chain as well so her body got stimulation. He was glad his dick was out of her mouth, because her scream was a beautiful thing to behold.

Setting a rougher pace, he rocked back and forth, her mouth sucking on him despite her tears. When he leaned back to put a finger in her cunt, he found her hot, wet, and ready. The sensation of her mouth was too good at the moment, so he held off, tormenting himself and her with almost coming. When he squeezed her breasts together, she cried out.

"Please..."

Fuck, it was too much. "Don't come yet, Anya. Do it while swallowing my seed."

He fucked her chest with six more hard strokes and shoved his dick as far into her mouth as he could. The sensation of heat, her strong sucking, and the desperate cries she made around his dick had his own orgasm crashing down, an amazing rush of energy that felt so damn good. Each spurt sent a new wave of satisfaction through him even as Anya writhed through her own orgasm beneath him.

He moved off her and lifted the edge of the mattress, pulling out the safety sheers. A few snips later the blood flow returned to her breasts in what had to be a painful rush. She grabbed her chest and gave him an accusing look. "That hurts!"

"What did you say?"

"I mean, um, Master, I—"

He gave her a stern look and removed the tweezer clamps from her nipples, earning a renewed round of yells. When he reached for her clit, she covered herself. "Oh no. Please no."

"Hands over your head, Anya."

"Please, Master. It is going to hurt."

"Yes, but it is also going to feel fantastic. Let go, Anya. You don't have a choice. I'm going to do whatever I want to you, and right now I want to play with your sore little clit."

She shivered but did as he asked with obvious reluctance.

"Spread your legs." She did but not far enough. He slapped her no doubt aching breast. "More."

This time she gave him enough room to lie down between her legs. The liquid arousal from her two orgasms was dripping out of her, leaking down the crack of her ass to the silk sheets beneath. The puffy skin of her labia was a nice hot pink color, but he wanted it red from being fucked.

Glancing up, he caught his reflection in the mirror and chided himself for being greedy. She'd earned a turn watching herself in the mirrors without anyone looking back but herself.

Rearing back on his haunches, his dick once again hardening, he smacked her thigh. "Stand up."

Giving him a confused look, she did as he asked. When he lay back, he motioned to her. "Come sit on my face."

Her knees trembled, and she stood over him, her wet pussy hovering right above his mouth. Then she knelt above him, a tentative movement that put her almost out of reach. "Now watch yourself in the mirrors. Don't look away. Don't close your eyes. See how fucking hot you are."

He reached up and unhooked the clit clamp. Her outraged scream turned to a wail as he pulled her down to his mouth and began to ever so softly lick her very swollen clit. The blood rushed back into the nub, and it quivered against his tongue before quickly hardening. Her arousal came almost faster than he could lick it up. She began to rock against his tongue, and he let her pleasure herself with his mouth, her shudders making his dick fill until it throbbed.

Swirling his tongue around the hard bundle of nerves, he paused to pull her butt cheeks apart. She certainly loved having her ass played with, and he was only too happy to oblige. When her little moans turned to cries, he stopped, blowing on her pussy. "Good girl. Now get on your hands and knees."

She scrambled off him and went on all fours, pushing her ass up into the air. The gold chain rolled on her waist, and the look she gave him, one filled with lust, made him lunge after her. He grasped the chain around her waist and jerked her backward. After grabbing the oil with his free hand, he dripped it down the slit of her buttocks.

"Hmm, pussy or ass, pussy or ass... Which one do I want to be in tonight?"

She arched in a pleasing curve. "Whatever Master wishes."

"Damn right."

He positioned himself at her pussy and thrust in with one long stroke, using the chain to keep her from jerking involuntarily away from him. She bucked against him, and he rode it out, not moving an inch out of her tight sheath, which gripped him despite the pain. He waited, giving her time to settle down, to absorb the feelings.

"Reach between your legs and play with your clit and my balls."

She went down so that her shoulders were resting on the mattress, her face to the side, before reaching between them. At the first flutter of her fingers against his balls, he groaned, trying to get in even deeper. To be inside her like no other man ever had.

Slowly her body loosened around him, and he pulled back in a long stroke while she continued to tease herself. Her erotic moans increased in volume, and she became restless beneath him, pushing herself back against his dick, taking everything he had. Barely moving, he stroked across her ass. "This is so pretty, so soft and perfect for fucking."

She whispered an encouragement as he began to work the oil he'd poured earlier into her bottom. Eager young thing that she was, she soon pushed back on his dick rough enough that he had to hold on to her. Who knew the little slip of a girl could give him such a rough ride.

Smacking her ass hard, he pulled out and leaned down. He grabbed one ass cheek and bit it, using enough force to leave an impression of his teeth. He wanted to watch that mark while he fucked her in the ass. That imprint was his alone.

After mounding some pillows together against the back of the sturdy medicine cabinet, he grabbed a tube of lube he'd set next to the bed earlier. Then he lay down and placed his arms behind his head. "I want you to ride me, reverse cowgirl. But I want to fuck your ass. You're going to be the one putting it in, impaling yourself on me. And I want you to watch yourself, because I'm sure as fuck going to be watching my cock disappear into that hot, tight young butt."

As she positioned herself over him, he grabbed the lube and covered his cock in a generous amount, wanting to give her only a little bit of pain. Her hair fell down over her breasts as she gripped the head of his dick in her small fist. Holding it to her butt, she looked at him in the mirror and began to slowly sink down. Bit by bit his body disappeared into hers. The strain showed on her face. How could anyone not be turned on by the mix of pleasure and pain, the hard-as-a-rock red nipples and gushing cunt? Anya loved it, and he loved giving it to her.

She reached the halfway point and paused, panting.

"Turn around."

Moving slowly, she did as he asked, managing not to lose him out of the tight clutch of her ass. The twisting motion made his testicles draw up, and he willed himself not to come.

As soon as she was facing him, he began to play with her nipples, coaxing small gasps from her pretty pink lips. Moving his hips, he rose up as she came down, both of them working to get him all the way in.

When she sat down all the way on his cock, they both gave a pained groan. He massaged her breasts, bringing the soreness back, playing with her still-swollen nipples. She placed her hands on his chest and moved her feet for better leverage, lowering and raising herself on his dick. Each stroke made his toes curl, but he focused on her pleasure, on holding out and enjoying her efforts to please him.

Abandoning one of her breasts, he moved his hand to her sopping-wet pussy. Her clit was a hard pearl among the soft flesh, easy to find and manipulate. Almost at once she froze on top of him, then began to fuck him harder.

"That's it, baby. Ride me."

She flexed her hips against his thumb, rubbing herself in a tight circular motion while slowly rising up. Now it was his turn to shout at the mind-blowing sensation. Unable to take it, he rolled them over so she was on her back. Forcing her legs up and wide, he fucked her with hard, deep strokes.

Tears began to fall from her eyes, and he leaned over, kissing them away while his body continued to punish her. She stiffened beneath him, then came with a long, loud cry. Her ass practically sucked the cum out of him, her strong contractions jerking him like a fist. He yelled out and gripped her hips, holding her still, making her take his cum.

The world grew fuzzy around the edges as the powerful orgasm left him feeling scoured from the inside out. Pulling as gently as he could out of Anya, he stood on unsteady legs and went back into his room so he could get to the sink. After cleaning himself, he soaked one towel in hot water and brought the cleansing herbal wipes. He also brought a little something extra he hoped Anya would like.

She was on her belly when he came back in, her legs akimbo and her breathing even and deep. Her subspace was something almost akin to sleep, where she just drifted. At least that's what she'd told him, that after a round of sex with him, she felt like she was floating in warm water, weightless and content.

Hating to disturb her mood but needing to take care of her, he cleaned her as gently as he could. The wipes made her whimper a bit, and he felt a twinge of guilt that he'd used her so hard. He hadn't meant to; it was just that when they were together, it felt natural to give her everything he had, as rough as she wanted. Even the bite mark on her ass that would become a bruise would be something she would see or touch and smile. He'd seen her do it often enough this week, brushing her hand over a spot he'd marked on her, a content smile curving her lips.

She was an absolute treasure.

"Anya, sit up, sweetheart."

She made a grumpy noise but didn't move.

"I need to give you your reward."

She giggled, an almost tipsy sound. "You just did."

"While I appreciate the flattery, I had something else in mind." He sat back on the pillows and hauled her against him so she sat between his thighs with her head resting against his shoulder, facing the mirrors.

Her reflection gave him a lazy smile. "You are so awesome."

Shaking his head, he rubbed his cheek against her, earning him a squeal as his beard scratched her. "I know. Anya, I want you to wear something, if you're willing."

"You know I'll do anything you want, Jesse. You only have to ask me."

Gathering his courage, he held up the black velvet ribbon in front of her. A two-carat pear-shaped diamond dangled from the antique platinum fastening on the ribbon.

She stiffened against him, her gaze going between his reflection in the mirror and the pendant. "Oh, Jesse, I couldn't."

"Listen to what I have to say first." He dropped the necklace into her hands, and she grabbed it reflexively. "This is a temporary collar. I would like you to wear it until you go to Paris."

Her lower lip trembled, and she looked up at him with tears in her eyes. "I don't want to go."

"Baby, you have to go."

"You don't want me here?"

He sighed, pulling her close and cuddling her. In his experience, submissives sometimes felt very vulnerable after an intense scene. "Of course I do, but I want you to go to Paris even more. And not because I don't want you. You need to go to Paris to figure out what you want."

She turned in his arms, seeking his gaze. "I want you."

The raw emotion in her voice tugged at his heart. "And I want you, but you still need to go to Paris. Anya, you've been planning this for years. Go, enjoy yourself. You only get an opportunity like this once in a lifetime. I want you to relish what the world has to offer. And if at the end of your time over there, you still want to be with me when you come home, we'll see how it works."

She curled into his arms and turned her face against his chest. "The thought of leaving you breaks my heart."

"Baby, don't say that. The time will pass before you know it. Maybe you'll meet some young French guy over there who will sweep you off your feet. Then I'll have to go find and kill him."

She giggled against him, but it was a fragile sound. "Can I wear this crystal necklace in Paris? If I have to be over there, I want everyone who looks at me to know who I belong to."

He opened his mouth to tell her it was a diamond, then shut it again. He didn't need her freaking out if anything happened to it. After all, it was just a rock. "Of course."

She held the pendant up to the light of the candles,

turning it back and forth. "It's very pretty. I, well, I mean, you don't have to do this at all, but I was kinda hoping that maybe if I waited for you, that you would wait for me? I mean, if you don't date anyone, I won't."

He nuzzled his face against her hair, breathing her in and savoring her warmth. "As if anyone could replace you."

"Is that a yes?"

"Yes, Anya. I won't date anyone else while you're in Paris as long as you do the same."

She let out a long, low breath, and he realized she'd been really worried about that.

"Have I given you some indication that I wanted to date other people?"

"Well, no, but look at you. Women have to be throwing themselves at your feet everywhere you go." She scowled. "Diane said something about you going out with a different woman every night."

He promised himself next time he saw his former sister-in-law they were going to sit down for a long chat. "Did you believe her?"

"Well, no. I'd seen you both Friday and Saturday that week, so I knew she was wrong."

He smiled and gently moved her off his lap. "Come on. Let me put your collar on, and we can go see if my mom and the boys are back yet with ice cream."

Her cheeks flooded with color, and she quickly stood. "Oh my goodness. How long have we been in here? Did they hear us?"

"No, this room is soundproofed. You can scream and cry all you want, and no one will hear you except me."

She fluttered her lashes at him before moving aside her braid so he could clasp the black velvet ribbon in place. Once it was on, he kissed the nape of her neck and watched the diamond sparkle in the hollow of her throat. She touched it and smiled up at him. "It's beautiful. I love it."

"I lov— I'm glad you like it."

She blinked, then turned away so he couldn't see her face. "Let's get dressed and go eat some ice cream. Then we can watch a movie with the boys and your mom."

He followed after her, wanting to jerk her back in his arms, plead with her not to go, but unable to get past his sense of right and wrong. And knowing he was doing the right thing didn't make letting Anya go any easier. Especially when he'd seen the joy in her eyes when he almost told her the truth.

He loved her.

CHAPTER FIFTEEN

The busy crowd at the entrance to the line to get through airport security flowed around Anya as she looked up at Jesse. A few feet away, her father was talking with Jesse's mother, still a little flustered at Anya's abrupt admission that she was dating her boss and that Jesse and his family would also be coming to say good-bye. Her father kept running his hand through his thinning gray hair, and her brothers weren't sure if they should be pissed or happy.

Jesse shifted against her, and all of it faded away. His intense brown gaze poured into her soul, and she wondered anew how she was ever going to manage without it. These last two weeks had been some of the happiest of her life. The thought of leaving him was killing her inside. The fact that he was making her go didn't help, leaving her at once sad and mad.

"Please, Jesse, one more month. I promise I'll go to Paris afterwards."

"Baby, you're killing me." He brushed her hair back from her cheek, pausing to cup her chin. "If I set you free and—"

"If you start quoting that stupid line about setting something free and if it comes back, it is meant to be, I'll kick you in the shins."

His lips twitched in a smile but didn't chase the sorrow from his own expression. "Don't be sassy with me, girl. You need the time in Paris in ways you'll understand when you're older."

"That's another thing. Just because you are older than me doesn't mean you know everything." She placed her hand over his heart, feeling the solid thump beneath her palm. "Why would I want to leave when you're all I've ever wanted?"

Taking her hand in his own, he brought it to his mouth and rubbed his lips against her knuckles. "Three months, Anya. I expect you to enjoy the wonders Paris has to offer, not sit in your apartment by yourself and pine away like some actress in an old romance movie. I expect you to send me pictures of the things you see, the places you go. Allow me to live there with you through your eyes."

She lifted her chin. "I may barely think about you when I'm over there."

This time his grin reached his eyes. "Well, I'll have to endeavor to find ways to remain in your thoughts."

"And that's another thing, why only e-mail? Why can't I call you?"

"Because I can't resist you, Anya. Even now I want to bundle you up and take you home with me, but that is absolutely the wrong thing to do. I want you, all of you, but I want you to understand what you would be giving up to be with me."

"I do understand, and I don't care!"

Jesse pulled her into his arms, resting his head on top of hers. "Easy, baby. Write to me, tell me about your adventures working with the French dancers, what fabulous food you got to eat that day, how you like the Louvre. Your letters will be the highlight of my day."

She buried her face against his chest. "Will you be going to Wicked without me?"

"Yes, but only to watch and be with friends. My heart is already spoken for."

With a deep sigh she pushed away from him and swallowed hard. "Okay, I have to go."

Holding her hand, he led her back to her family so she could make her good-byes. She managed to hold her tears back until it was Teddy's and Mark's turns to hug her. They didn't quite understand what was going on, only that Anya would be gone for a long time. She loved them as much as she loved Jesse, and when they cried because they were going to miss her, she couldn't help the tears that flowed down her face.

Jesse carefully pulled her away and gave her a gentle, devastating kiss before handing her the sheet of paper with her flight information on it. All too soon she found herself alone in the security line, trying to wipe away her tears with the sleeve of her shirt while the people around her pretended not to notice. The rest of the journey to her terminal went by in a blur, her mind too stuffed with thoughts and her heart aching in her chest.

She'd arrived in plenty of time to catch her flight, so she sat down and stared out the window, seeing nothing and not really thinking anything either. It was a state akin to being in subspace but emptier. Instead of being surrounded by pleasure in the depths of her soul, she floated alone in the sky. Cupping her hands to her nose, she could still smell him on her skin.

—✳—

Anya looked out the window of her taxi taking her through the streets of Paris, her sorrow momentarily pushed aside by the beauty of the city. She was on her way to her home for the summer and practically had her nose pressed to the window of the cab as they drove past all the places she'd dreamed of seeing. Part of her wanted to tell the cab driver to stop right now so she could get out and walk around the city, but she had her suitcase and carry-on still with her. Most of her clothing had been shipped over earlier and should be waiting for her at the flat she was renting in the theater district off Rue de Richelieu.

The traffic in this section of the city was insane, and she listened with half an ear as her taxi driver cursed beneath his breath when he narrowly avoided hitting the car in front of them. They were getting closer to the heart of the city, and Anya's anticipation increased until she was fidgeting in her seat. All her years of hard work, all her studying and busting her ass learning her craft had finally paid off.

If only Jesse were here, it would be perfect.

The tears started to well up again, but she swallowed hard and blinked them back. No, she wasn't going to cry in front of strangers. Later, when she was alone in her apartment, she'd have her breakdown.

The cab driver pulled up to the curb on the narrow street they were on and said to her in French, "Here we are."

Thanking her grandmother for taking the time to teach her French, she replied, "Thank you so much."

After retrieving her possessions from the back of the cab, she stood on the sidewalk before the elegant building that was to be her home for the next three months. Located within walking distance of the Opéra Comique, where she'd be doing her internship, the white-painted building with its beautiful black wrought-iron balconies looking out into the street took her breath away.

Anya had Jesse to thank for finding this place for her. On her own Anya would have ended up in some student ghetto on the outskirts of Paris, but Jesse had made sure she was in the best place possible. Before Anya forgot, she took out her phone and snapped a picture of the front of the building for him.

A flower shop occupied the main floor of the building, and bright tulips of every color sat in a raised metal bucket outside the front door. Anya turned so she could take pictures up and down the street, making note of the coffeehouse nearby and a bakery. When she turned back, a lovely woman with salt-and-pepper hair and dressed in an elegant blue summer dress hailed her from the entrance to the flower shop.

"Hello, are you Anya Kozlov?"

Shoving her phone back in her purse, Anya nodded. "Hello. You must be Claudette."

The woman came down the steps and made her way over

the sidewalk to where Anya still stood with her luggage. Claudette gave her a kiss on either cheek, the smell of earth and plants drifting from her. "Your French is wonderful. Welcome to Paris, Anya."

"Thank you so much. My grandmother grew up near the Parc des Buttes-Chaumont before she moved to the United States in the 1960s."

The women chatted about Paris as Claudette led her up the narrow steps to the second level of the building. According to her, Paul, the owner of the building and a banker, lived on the third floor, while Claudette occupied most of the second. They kept the old servant quarters as a rental, which was where Anya would be staying.

They reached the door to Anya's apartment, and Claudette handed Anya her key. "I'll give you a few moments to settle in while I go get Paul. He's eager to meet you."

"Thank you."

She slipped the key into the lock while Claudette walked back the way they'd come, her heels clicking on the polished wood floors. Taking a deep breath, Anya turned the key and opened the door to her flat. At the first sight of her new home, she couldn't help but smile at the huge vase of pink roses sitting on a small breakfast table.

Wheeling her luggage into the room, she closed the door behind her and looked around. The flat was only two rooms, a main room that was her living room/bedroom/kitchen, and a bathroom off to the right. The glass double doors leading to her balcony let plenty of sunshine into the room, making the polished oak floors gleam. The kitchenette was modern and updated, but miniscule. A full-size bed sat against the right wall, while to her left a couch and coffee table took up most of the room.

Though this apartment was small by American standards, for Paris this was a luxurious flat. She wondered if Jesse had lied about how much this place cost. The amount she was paying in rent wasn't near enough to cover the cost of staying here. Heck, when she'd been looking for a place to stay on her own, she'd looked in this section of the city but couldn't find anything for under four thousand euros a month.

As she walked farther into the room, she traced her fingers over the beautiful roses and walked to the double doors, peeking out into the busy street below. Her balcony had pretty blue and purple flowers hanging from the planter on the railing, and she grinned in pure delight.

She was here, in Paris. Like for real.

A knock at the door startled her, and she yelled out, "Come in."

The door opened, and a handsome man with dark hair and a neatly trimmed mustache entered, followed by Claudette holding a bottle of wine and a tray of what looked like cheese. He gave Anya an open and friendly smile before crossing the room and kissing her on either cheek. "Anya, welcome to Paris. Jesse has told me so much about you.'"

Anya smiled up at him. "Thanks for renting this place to me. It is amazing."

Claudette moved into the kitchen and pulled a bottle opener out of one of the drawers near the sink. "I know it's barely past breakfast, but I thought you might like a glass of wine and a nibble after your long flight. Do you like chardonnay?"

They settled down in her small sitting area, laughing and talking about the city and Paul's visits to the United States. Anya was on her third glass of wine when Claudette leaned forward and held her hand out toward Anya's throat. "May I?"

For a moment Anya didn't know what she meant, then nodded. "Sure."

Claudette lifted the dangling crystal and let out a soft whistle. "It is exquisite."

"Thank you. My Ma—my boyfriend gave it to me." She swallowed hard, suddenly missing Jesse something fierce. This would be so much better if he was sitting next to her, no doubt charming the pants off Claudette and Paul. While Anya had experienced homesickness before, the cold and hollow feeling in her chest was more like the superplague version of being homesick. She didn't just miss her family and the States; she missed the man who held the other half of her heart.

Anya looked away and tried to wipe a tear that had managed to escape without the other two noticing. Great, get a couple of glasses of wine in her, and she turned into a weepy mess.

Claudette smiled while Paul gave her an odd look. "He has good taste. Is he as handsome as he is generous?"

Anya wasn't quite sure what to make of that, or if her drink-befuddled mind had even translated the other woman's words properly. "He is... Wait, I have some pictures of him on my phone."

She moved closer to Paul and Claudette, then began to show them images of Jesse. By the time she reached the last one, a picture she had taken of Jesse in his leathers with his shirt off, getting ready to ravish her, she was barely able to hold back a full-on breakdown.

Claudette made a low sound of approval. "Oh my. He certainly is deliciously male. If the men in the States look like that, I may have to book a trip myself."

Paul reached out and patted Anya's shoulder. "Now, now. No tears. While I'd be crying myself to sleep if I had that waiting back at home for me, I know your Mas—your boyfriend wouldn't approve of you being sad."

Scrunching down her brow, Anya looked closer at Paul. "Thank you." She tried to figure out how to ask him something without outing him in front of Claudette. Fingering her collar, she looked into Paul's eyes. "He takes very good care of me."

Claudette looked down at the watch on her wrist. "Shit. Time has gotten away from me. I'm afraid I must return to my shop. Anya, if you're not busy tonight, I'd love to take you out to dinner and show you around Paris after you've had a chance to rest."

They all stood, and Anya nodded. "That would be very much appreciated."

Claudette left first with a promise to meet up with Anya down at her flower shop later. Paul waited until the other woman had left and turned back to Anya.

"I don't know if Jesse mentioned it, but I'm in the BDSM lifestyle as well."

Leaning against her kitchen counter to keep from swaying after her overindulgence in wine, Anya stared at him. "No, he didn't."

"If you ever want to go to Wicked's sister club, Misericorde, please let me know. It would be my honor to take you as my guest."

Anya crossed her arms. "Thank you, but I have a Master."

Laughing, Paul shook his head. "You misunderstand. I'm a submissive as well. I'd be much more likely to be hitting on your handsome Master than you. Jesse is friends with one of the Doms I like to play with at Misericorde. "

It took her a second to process that, and when she did, a hot flush burned through her. "Oh, oh. I'm sorry. I didn't mean to offend you."

"Not at all." He gave her a smile that had a hint of sadness in it. "Not many people know that I am gay, so if you could keep it between us, I would appreciate it. Claudette knows, of course, but I try to keep my love life private."

Growing more tired by the second, Anya nodded, then yawned. "Of course."

"Look at me, babbling on while you're practically falling asleep standing up. You get some rest, and when you're ready, I'd be more than happy to take you to Misericorde and beat off the Doms that will no doubt flock to you."

She slipped off her shoes and yawned again. "I'd like that."

"Excellent." He opened the door, then looked over his

shoulder. "By the way, the flowers are from your Master."

As soon as he closed the door behind him, she moved across her flat to where the roses stood on the table. Brushing her fingers over the silky-soft petals, she no longer tried to hold back her tears. Stumbling over to her bed, she threw herself on the mattress, clutched a pillow close to her, and cried from the unbearable loneliness of missing her Master.

———✦———

Six hours later she woke as the sun was beginning to set. Though the buildings across the street blocked most of the skyline, she could still see the bright pink burning the clouds outside of her window. She got out of bed, washed her face, and brushed her teeth, then set up her brand-new laptop on the small table near the roses. The computer had been a gift from Jesse, and he'd promised her that no matter where she was in the world, she'd be able to e-mail him.

Her massive cry earlier had left her feeling calmer, a little more in control. Mercifully, the wine hadn't left her with a headache, and her stomach rumbled at the thought of food. A quick glance at the time assured her she'd be able to write Jesse before going down to meet Claudette. For a moment she considered telling Jesse how much she missed him, how much she wished he was here, but she decided instead to try and bring him joy with her words instead of sorrow.

Dear Jesse,

I finally made it to Paris, in a much better mood than when you saw me last. Part of that was because of my upgrade to first class. A totally unnecessary but very much appreciated gift from you. I had no idea they had actual beds you could sleep in with your own little private cubicle. It certainly made resting easier so when I arrived in France I was more than awake.

Jesse, Paris…Paris is amazing.

The city fairly hums with energy, everyone bustling about.

I've never been in a place where so many people walk and ride bikes. I was nervous about not having a car, but there is seriously no place to park in the section of Paris where my flat is. My flat is situated above a flower shop owned by my neighbor, Claudette. She is very nice, as is Paul. They both welcomed me to the city with wine, flowers, bread, and cheese.

Very surreal for a girl from Nowheresville, Indiana.

Tomorrow I'll be going to the burlesque theater to begin my study with them. I'm very nervous, scared even, but I'll be wearing your collar, and you'll be there with me, giving me strength.

Your Anya

Dear Jesse,

I can't believe a month has already passed! I've been so busy trying to do as you ordered, to live life to the fullest over here. Last night I finally got up the nerve to go dancing with the ladies from the show, and I had a blast. You should have seen how those women flirted with the men, leading them on and driving them crazy but letting the men get away with nothing. They are trying to teach me how to dance, but I'm afraid I'll never be able to do more than shuffle in time to the beat.

I think about you at night when I'm alone in my bed.

I miss you.

Your Anya

Dear Jesse,

Sorry it's taken me so long to get back to you. The past three days have gone by in a blur. You know that banker that owns the building, Paul? Well, his family runs a wonderful vineyard not too far from Paris, and he took me for a visit. He brought me to meet his family as his cover so they'd get off his back about finding a wife. You know, pretty foreign girl, long-distance relationship, and all of that. Anyways, he's also a submissive, and he offered to show me around the Parisian

BDSM clubs. I turned him down because going there, seeing the Masters with their women, it would only make me miss you more than ever.

But back onto a happier subject because I know you don't want me moping around all the time. You would have loved the train ride out of the city. Someday when we return together I'd like to take you to the wine region and spend a week going from vineyard to vineyard. And don't bother to write back saying that I never know what I'll want in four weeks, because I will still want you just as much then as I do now.

That hasn't changed for me, Master. The more people I'm around, the more of the world I see, the more I realize how much I care about you. Oh, I certainly miss the way you dominate me, and no man can hold a candle to you in the looks department, but I miss talking with you. I miss waking up in your arms, safe and secure against you as you hold me in your sleep.

I'm going to go before I start crying again. Give the boys kisses for me.

Your Anya

Dear Jesse,

It is one week until I return to the States, and you seem to have vanished off the face of the earth. Please e-mail me and let me know you're okay. I haven't heard from you in three days, and I'm worried. Yeah, I know, you were worried when you didn't hear from me for three days when I was caught up in the craziness of opening week at the burlesque theater, but we both know that you're the responsible one. I'm the flighty seamstress who almost got arrested for indecent exposure.

If you want to know the story on that one, you're going to have to spank it out of me. And yes, I realize this is brat behavior, topping from the bottom to try and get a punishment, but holy hell, do I miss you. You've invaded my dreams almost every night, and I still sleep in your T-shirts that I "borrowed" from you.

So please, please e-mail me back. If you don't, I'm going to call you even though you forbid it. Then you'll have to punish me for that as well. Plus you won't know what your surprise is.

Your Anya

She picked up her phone and scrolled through to Jesse's cell phone number before walking out onto her small terrace. The early morning sun shone down on the busy street scene below her of people selling flowers and produce. Her neighbor, Claudette, was down there right now, and Anya wondered if the older woman wanted to go get coffee later. After spending nearly three months living next door to the vibrant middle-aged woman, she'd miss their conversations over wine about life and love.

Removing her thumb from the Send button, she turned her phone off and sighed. No doubt Jesse had his reasons for his silence, but she'd done exactly what he wanted and now she wanted her reward. Doubt tried to wiggle its way into her heart, and she wondered if this was his way of breaking things off with her.

No, that didn't make sense.

Every one of his letters had been filled with warmth and humor, rays of sunlight into her day that warmed her from the inside out. Of course he'd be waiting for her after she got off the flight back in DC. Just because he didn't immediately respond to her letters like usual didn't mean anything. He could be very busy with work, or maybe something came up with the boys.

Or maybe he'd found someone he liked better.

She tucked her hair behind her ear and looked around her small junk drawer for a rubber band to tie it back with. She'd gotten it trimmed by a woman who did the dancers' hair for the theater. Now, instead of falling in a straight sheaf down her back, it had layers and framed her face. It was still long enough to reach her lower back, but it had more style now.

She hoped Jesse liked it.

As she got ready to go grab some breakfast downstairs, she slipped on her pale pink high heels and grinned. One of the first things she'd gotten used to was wearing her high heels. Women in Paris wore them almost everywhere, and she'd gotten quite good at walking in them. Hell, she could even run in them now.

A knock came from her door, followed by a male voice. "*J'ai des fleurs pour vous.*"

Her heart lightened as she wondered if Jesse had sent her some flowers. He did that pretty often and each time with a wonderful note. "*Une momento, s'il vous plait.*"

Grabbing her purse from the counter, she dug around and got out a tip before opening the door.

"*Mettez-vous les fleurs sur la table, s'il vous plait.*"

Standing on the other side with an armful of pink roses wrapped in gray velvet stood Jesse.

She inhaled sharply, unable to believe what she was seeing. Jesse couldn't be here. He was in America...and yet here he stood, his cologne scenting the air between them. He wore a pair of jeans that hugged his hips and a stylish black button-down shirt. When her gaze reached his face again, he smiled and handed her the roses.

"These reminded me of you."

"Jesse?"

"Are you going to invite me in?"

She tossed the roses into the room, then flung herself at him, the momentum pushing him back against the plaster wall of the hallway. A moment later he wrapped his arms around her and lifted her to his mouth, her toes dangling off the floor and her hands buried in his hair. Warm, solid, alive, he was really here.

Their tongues met, dancing and tangling with each other until she didn't know where he ended and she began. With a soft growl, Jesse tore his mouth from hers. She reached for him but had to grip his shoulders when he wrapped her legs around his waist and carried her back into her flat.

"You're still wearing your collar."

"I never took it off, Master."

He kicked the door closed and began to kiss her again, then slammed her into the wall. Holding her there with his chest and stomach, he reached down and twisted her panties over to the side. When he thrust a finger inside her, she cried out, and he hissed.

"Fuck, baby. You're so tight. You haven't put anything inside that little pussy since you left, have you?"

Trying to rock herself on his fingers, she shook her head. "Wanted to wait for you."

"Mmm, but you have gotten off while you've been here. I'm sure of it. Did you use your fingers or do you have a toy?"

Her ability to speak fled as he shuttled his fingers in and out of her aching body in a rhythm that swiftly drove her crazy. Her entire body tensed, and she throbbed so close to the edge she could almost feel the first blissful release of her orgasm.

Before she could fully go over, he removed his hand and left her straining. "Bad girl. Am I going to have to train you all over again?"

"Master, please. I've missed you so much."

His gaze softened, and he slowly lowered her legs to the ground. "Not as much as I've missed you. Now go present yourself on your bed for me."

She did as he asked, removing her clothes while he pulled the curtains enough to hide her but still light the room. Seeing him prowl around, touch her things, and smile made her heart so full she could barely breathe. A small smile tickled her lips as she realized Jesse would finally see the surprise she'd done for him.

After looking at a bottle of wine on her counter, he started to return to her, then came to an abrupt stop. Unable to hide her smile, she looked down and tried to keep from giggling. Oh, she would have loved to see his face when he spotted the gold ring now piercing the hood of her clit, but she didn't want to give him any excuse to punish her. Besides, etched into the ball holding the ring together was the letter J.

"When did you get that done?" His voice was thick with desire.

"Right after I arrived. One of the girls at Wicked had hers done, and the way she talked about it and how much her Master loved it made me want one. I knew I'd need some healing time, so I decided that if I didn't get it done now, I never would."

"Am I correct in assuming the J on your clit ring is for Jesse?"

"Yes, Master."

He chuckled and stroked her thigh. "Baby, it's beautiful. Now lie back so I can get a better look."

Only too eager to get that marvelous mouth where she needed him the most, she did as he asked and spread her legs wide, giving him the unimpeded view she knew he liked. Holding her gaze, he quickly stripped out of his clothes, his big dick pointing up past his belly button once he was fully naked. At the sight of his cock, her whole body clenched with need, and he made a low, growling noise.

"Remember, no coming until I say."

"Yes, Master." She would try, she really would, but she didn't think anything could stop her from coming once he touched her.

He crawled up the bed toward her, all menacing male power. When he lowered himself to his elbows between her legs, her breath caught in her throat. He looked at her pussy for a long time before fingering the little ring. "Show me how you like to use it."

Eager to please him, knowing how much he liked to watch her play, she reached between her legs and began to gently tug at the ring, then roll her clit with it. He leaned down and began to lick her fingers, his tongue swiping her clit. She froze, a hard tremble nearly undoing her.

"Keep touching yourself, Anya."

She wanted to scream at him, to grab him by the back of his head, to force him to finish her, but she knew she couldn't. He was so much bigger than her, stronger. God, that was a turn-on. When she began to rub her pussy lips, his tongue was there, licking in between her fingers, sucking on her tender flesh, biting her.

He moved her fingers back to her clit; his tongue followed. She arched when he hooked the ring with his tongue and tugged, her toes curling as she tried with all her might not to come.

"Anya, come for me."

With a scream that tore from deep in her belly, she convulsed against his mouth, writhing beneath him as he continued to lick and suck her while she came. She clutched his head to her pussy, rocking her lips and shaking when he latched his mouth over her sex and shoved his tongue deep inside. He was greedy about eating her pussy, drinking down every drop of honey her body gave him and demanding more.

Once he'd wrenched a final shudder from her, he moved up her body, pausing at her breasts. With a feral look in his eyes, he bit the mounds of her breasts, hard enough to leave marks. Each sharp pain, then release seemed to tug at her clit from the inside, rousing her again. When he reached her nipples, she tensed, then moaned when he began to suckle first one, then the other while he massaged the sore spots on her breasts.

The combination of pleasure and pain had her begging him to fuck her, to fill her up, to take away her loneliness. She confessed how much she missed him, how much he meant to her, and how happy she was that he was finally here.

"If this is a dream, Master, I don't want to wake up."

Leaving her breasts in an aching, deliciously sore state, he moved to her mouth and placed a kiss there that conveyed his love for her and how much he'd missed her. He kissed her like she was the most precious thing in the world. Pushing up onto his arms, he looked down at her. There was such warmth mixed with his desire that her chest constricted even as her body cried out for him. With his shoulders bunched up, the hard muscles of his arms standing out in sharp relief, and her scent covering his mouth, he had to be the sexiest man she'd ever seen.

Reaching between them, he placed his cock at her entrance, the fine lines around his eyes tightening. She rubbed herself against him, not able to get any farther than the broad head barely penetrating her because of his fist. Looking down between their bodies, she moaned with need at the sight of her swollen pussy against his fist.

"Anya, look at me."

Their gazes met, and erotic lighting burned a path through her body. Removing his hand, he began to slowly penetrate her tight sheath. "Anya, I love you."

Tears burned her eyes. She hugged him as tightly as she could. "I love you too."

Together they began to move, a sensual glide that took her breath away. She refused to let him go, keeping their bodies pressed tight together while she kissed his face, his neck, any part of him she could reach. His languid motions took him farther into her body, bumping that part deep within that sent chills skating up and down her spine. He groaned and increased his tempo, their stomachs meeting with a slap, and she pulled him down for a kiss.

The ring in her clit pulled, rubbed, and tugged with each of his thrusts, making it feel like he was playing with her tender bud even as he pinned her hands down to the bed. Putting pressure on her wrists, he pounded into her, that hard, unyielding thrust she loved so much. Her body tightened into a delicious coil of pleasure, the need for release making her wanton beneath him. She whispered all the dirty, wicked things she would do for him if he would only let her come.

His thrusts became ragged, and his grip on her wrists

increased to the point of pain. She reveled in the additional sensations mixing with her passion, turning into something explosive.

"Go ahead, baby," Jesse said in a tight, strained voice. "Come with me."

Grinding her pelvis against his, her back arching even as he kept her arms pinned to the bed, she came with a harsh snap of her hips, her body shaking as he bellowed and emptied himself into her with strong jerks of his cock. The orgasm took her down into the deep pool of pleasure she'd missed so much, the warm floating in the darkness only Jesse could give her.

He collapsed on top of her, rolling them onto their side without leaving the tight clutch of her pussy. Little aftershocks tightened her around him, and each time he groaned and twitched. Nuzzling closer to him, burying her face against his chest, she let out a sigh of such length that he chuckled.

"I missed you too, baby. More than you know."

He stroked her hair, her face, every bit of her body he could reach. He touched her with love and devotion, his energy cocooning her and making her his. She stirred against him and looked up at his face, unable to help what she was sure was a big cheesy grin.

"Hi, Master. It's nice to see you."

"Mmm, nice to see you too, Anya." He shifted, and his cock began to harden within her again. "I couldn't stay away any longer."

"Thank God."

"You are so precious to me. I don't want to be separated from you like that again."

"If you try to send me on another trip to make me see the world without you, I'll choke you myself."

He made an almost purring sound and rocked his hips against her, the now hard length of him sliding over her still-swollen tissues. "I promise you'll never be alone again."

Unable to stop her eyes from closing because of the

sensations he was drawing forth from her, she rubbed her lips against his neck. "That's all I want."

As the morning sunlight faded to the golden hue of later afternoon, they made love over and over until Anya didn't know where Jesse ended and she began.

Just the way she liked it.

THE END

ANN MAYBURN

Ann is Queen of the Castle to her wonderful husband and three sons in the mountains of West Virginia. In her past lives she's been an import broker, a communications specialist, a US Navy civilian contractor, a bartender/ waitress, and an actor at the Michigan Renaissance Festival. She also spent a summer touring with the Grateful Dead-though she will deny to her children that it ever happened.

From a young age she's been fascinated by myths and fairytales, and the romance that often was the center of the story. As Ann grew older and her hormones kicked in, she discovered trashy romance novels. Great at first, but she soon grew tired of the endless stories with a big, wonderful, emotional buildup to really short and crappy sex. Never a big fan of purple prose (throbbing spears of fleshy pleasure and wet honey pots make her giggle), she sought out books that gave the sex scenes in the story just as much detail and plot as everything else without using cringe worthy euphemisms. This led her to the wonderful world of erotic romance, and she's never looked back.

Now Ann spends her days trying to tune out cartoons playing in the background to get into her 'sexy space' and has learned to type one handed while soothing a cranky baby.

CPSIA information can be obtained at www.ICGtesting.com
Printed in the USA
LVOW10s2125100914

403527LV00001B/51/P